MW00465062

REESE T. LIGHTFOOT

DEVOTION FOR MY DEMONS

ART BY: OLGA BRINDAR

WORKBOOK PRESS LLC
187 E Warm Springs Rd,
Suite B285, Las Vegas, NV 89119, USA

Website:	https://workbookpress.com/
Hotline:	1-888-818-4856
Email:	admin@workbookpress.com

Ordering Information:
Quantity sales. Special discounts are available on quantity purchases by corporations, associations, and others.
For details, contact the publisher at the address above.

ISBN-13:   978-1-954753-34-1 (Paperback Version)
             978-1-954753-35-8 (Digital Version)

REV. DATE: 05/03/2021

I
Sweets

It's a tale as old as time.

You've heard it before, I'm sure. Boy meets girl, they fall in love, eventually get hitched and pop out a couple of kids, buy a house in the suburbs and work forty-plus hours a week until life starts to lose its luster and a full night of sleep belongs to some other couple that hasn't landed in the cohabitation trap ... yet. It's the same as every story of every couple that ever fell in love, right?

Little did I know, the day met Marie, my whole world would be flipped upside down. My life ended up so very far from the normal that I had always expected. But hey, when life gives you lemons, you make lemonade. Even if the lemons have infernal magic and will probably bite you.

But hang on, I'm getting ahead of myself, which is what I always do when I'm trying to get a story out too fast. Why don't I begin at the beginning?

Let me introduce myself. My name is Tyler Pine. My life was pretty standard issue. I was born in the eighties, just an average Black kid with a dash of geek in him – well, maybe more than a dash. In middle school I was picked on: I had a mouth full of braces and not enough Pokémon cards. I played an unhealthy amount of video games and watched an even unhealthier amount of anime.

High school was pretty much the same, except I started liking girls. I was also blessed with lots of colorful names, tripped, stuffed in lockers, and found myself on the receiving end of speedo-wedgies and endless female rejections. But then, senior year hit. I grew taller, got my braces off, hit the gym, and became a pro with computers. I even learned to play sports. I transformed into a phoenix!

Eventually, I was in college, doing what all college kids do: working hard and partying harder. Life was pretty damn good. But I was missing something. Or someone.

And then it happened: I met her, the girl of my dreams.

There she was at this frat party, standing next to a counter stacked with empty Miller Lites and handles of bottom-shelf gin and vodka. I wanted to talk to her, but I was speechless. Paralyzed where I stood, like a roach that had fallen into a freezer.

"Yo man, she is looking at you." It was my best friend Justin Cheeks, sipping on a screwdriver and grinning at me. "Go holla, bro."

Sure, easy for him to say. Justin had been my friend since time began; the yin to my yang. I liked comics, he liked sports. I liked anime, he only liked movies where something was exploding in the first five minutes. I liked to game, and he liked the gym. But he had my back since day one, loyal to the end.

"Man, if you don't talk to her, I will!"

Ah, the joys of peer pressure. I had to make my move, and quickly. Besides, the smell of cheap vodka and orange juice wafting out of his plastic cup was making me ill.

"Okay, okay."

"'Okay,' what?" Justin coaxed.

"I'm going in!"

What am I doing? I thought. *I'm not this kind of guy, I can't just walk up and TALK to her. Abort, abort!* But it was too late -- while my brain was looking for excuses to bail, my feet had already brought

9

me to her side. "Hi."

Oh god, I thought. *Did you just lead with "Hi?"* She turned to look at me. I found myself speechless again.

"Hey." Her blue-green eyes fixed on me as if she was examining my insides. I thought she was perfect: around five-foot-seven, she was wearing a flared skirt with an army green jacket. Everything about her seemed too cool for me. I wondered what had possessed me to walk up to her.

"I'm Tyler," I managed to reply, "And you are?"

She picked up the bourbon bottle on the coffee table next to us and swigged right out of the neck. I noticed it said cask-strength on the label.

"Ashi," she replied, seemingly unfazed by the liquor. "Marie Harley Ashi." As if on cue, Kanye's "Mercy" started up for the fifteenth time that night, the Dust Beagle intro sample echoing in my skull. *Wow, this girl just gave me the "Bond, James Bond",* I thought. So, I did what any guy would do next. I asked a stupid question.

"So, what brings you to this party?" I shouted over the music.

Smooth move, Tyler. But heck, I couldn't think, and my head was hurting from the combination of Miller Lite and the pounding of the subwoofer.

"Well, it was either go out with my friends or sit at home and eat a mango on the couch," she replied. *Odd,* I thought, but I pressed on with the conversation.

"So, what do you do for a living?" I asked. I had nothing at this point. But I had to stay in the game.

"I'm a nurse, actually. Freshly graduated!" she replied with a smile.

Now I had something. It was clear she was passionate about this. I asked her to tell me more. Before I knew it, those first seconds of my awkward start had turned into minutes of easily flowing conversation, and gradually, those minutes became hours. The night flew by as I found myself pouring my heart out to this stranger. Never in my short, geeky existence had I had such great conversation with another life form on this planet, besides my pet iguana – but he mostly just listened, anyway. This had to be it; this had to be the girl for me.

Before I knew it, the party was over, and we were sitting on the steps talking, joking and enjoying the night sky. Then it happened. The one thing any guy could ever hope for; that's right, the magic. Marie looked at me and tilted her head, smiling softly. I jerked my hand toward hers clumsily, and our fingers intertwined -- not my most graceful moment. I wondered if she was turned off by my obvious nervousness. I felt my heart pounding – it was a metronome swinging back and forth at 140 beats per minute.

Do I ask for a kiss? Ahh, I'm doing it again, overthinking it. I leaned in and our lips met with a peck. I immediately pulled back, wondering if I had screwed up. But her eyes drew me back in, reassuring me for a more passionate kiss. She smelled faintly sweet and tangy, like tropical fruit, and her lips were so soft. I didn't want the moment to end.

It wasn't every night I found myself lying in a stranger's bed staring at a popcorn ceiling – far from it. This was incredible. Sure, she had roommates, and the tacky tie-dye curtains were a bit much, not to mention I was sure she didn't wash her sheets on a strict seven-day cycle like I did, but hell, it felt as perfect as I had ever known.

That night was the beginning of something great: dates, movies, dinners, ice cream in the park, the whole nine yards. Before I knew it, we had been dating for a month. Still no official title, though, until one of our park dates one afternoon.

"So, Mr. Pine," said Marie, peeling an orange as we sat in the grass, "What do you want out of this?"

Coyly, I answered, "What do you mean?"

"Like, what do you want out of us?" Marie said.

Okay, I thought, *this is the moment. Don't mess up.*

"I want you," I said, swallowing a fearful gulp, hoping we were on the same page. She looked back at me with those odd-colored eyes, saying nothing. I realized she was waiting for more. *Come on, you idiot. Use your words.* "I mean I want us to be official, like an item." I paused. "How about you?"

"That's what I want," Marie replied. "I want us to grow, learn from each other, I want us to be happy, and I want you to be happy." Wow, I hadn't seen that coming. "I want you to meet my family, I want to meet your family, and I want a future."

And there it was, folks. The rest was history.

* * *

"Goddamnit! THIS HOUSE IS A MESS! Tyler, did the kids eat?"

"No," I replied.

"Did the dog go out?"

"NO!"

"Where is the soap we just bought?" yelled Marie.

"How should I know?!" I said with a huff.

"Dad, dad, dad, DAD!"

"What, what, what, WHAT?!" My youngest child, Logan, was tugging at my leg as if with each pull a bell should ring.

"DAD!"

"YES, boy," I replied, clenching my teeth.

"Bronx is in the trash again!"

"BRONX! GET OUT OF THE TRASH!" I screamed as I ran

down the steps, still half-dressed.

"Tyler, have you seen my stethoscope?" came Marie's frantic voice again. "I have to be out of here by 6:40 at the latest!"

Great, leave me with these little monsters, I thought.

"Dad, where is the PlayStation controller?" My older child, Harley, a wolverine stuck in the body of a six-year-old, was only concerned with video games. That is, when she wasn't gleefully causing chaos.

Somehow, over the last seven years, I had slowly slipped into the routine of family life. Every day was like Groundhog Day: wake up, get the kids ready, feed the dog, go to work. You know, the typical American Dream. And like everything else in my life, work was slowly but surely becoming a grand pleasure. I worked in IT at a local college, where I spent most of my days fixing computers, managing cables, and preventing professors from losing their data and freaking out. My boss managed to bust my balls twice a day, sometimes three if she was feeling generous. Traffic to work was a resort: an hour-long drive trapped in a gas-sucking vehicle set to the symphony of highway traffic. It truly was the creme de la creme.

Not even three minutes into my workday, my boss called me into her office. *Oh boy, looks like I get to listen to the great Professor Natalie White today,* I thought, turning the knob to her office.

"Tyler, we need to talk about a few things," she hissed as I sat down. "Your performance as of late is, well... It's not up to par."

I sat back in my chair and tried to make myself comfortable. This was going to be white-collar torture; I had endured it before, I would live through it again. I wondered where my job description ranked on the list of the world's most stressful jobs. Surely air traffic controllers weren't being given a verbal beat-down by their bosses as often as I was. But at least I could be sure that no one would die because of a mistake I made while on the clock.

Natalie opened her mouth to continue but was interrupted by the ring of her desk phone. *Salvation*, I thought. My mind started to wander as she took the call, but I was brought back to reality with her next words.

"Um yes, sure, he's actually right here," said Natalie.

Wait, what? Me?

Natalie pushed her sliding glasses up the bridge of her nose and sighed. "You may want to take this," she said.

I got a strange feeling in the pit of my stomach. My hand grew clammy as I reached for the phone.

"Hello?" I said, haltingly.

It was Marie. She needed me to leave work immediately. Her father, Dave, wasn't doing well. I hoped he was okay. Selfishly, I figured that at least it would help me dodge Natalie's verbal assault for the time being.

Damn, it felt good to be out of that office. I grabbed my bag and dashed to my car. Before I could even get in my phone rang. It was Marie again.

"Where are you?" she whispered.

"I'm coming; how's the old man?"

Her voice faltered, "Just get here, okay."

"I'm on my way."

Marie was daddy's little girl. During my drive I found myself imagining worst case scenarios. If Dave passed away, Marie and her siblings were going to be crushed. All of that meant an unbearable amount of consoling, cuddling under fuzzy blankets, and Marie going through boxes of tissues while I played the perfect one-man support system. I dimly remembered a time when I was a regular Don Juan with Marie. And I mean flowers, chocolates, balloons, and teddy bears – the whole nine. I even sat through a girly movie or two. Seven years and two children later, I was practically an android, totally desensitized to any emotions – the well was dry.

Ugh, let's hope it's just a really bad cold! Like a really, really bad cold!

It was time to get into model-supportive-spouse mode. As I pulled up to the hospital, I was greeted by Marie's uncle Nick. Uncle Nick was a strange bird. In fact, he wasn't really Marie's uncle at all. He worked with Dave at the auto shop, though in what capacity had always been a mystery to me. Plus, I was pretty sure he was drunk ninety-nine percent of the time. I was thinking about how much I wasn't looking forward to interacting with him when I looked up and realized he was already knocking on my window.

"Tyler, Tyler!"

Reluctantly, I rolled the window down. "Hey Nick," I said, concealing a weary sigh.

"Mmmmhh, did you hear?" Nick drunkenly uttered.

"Yes, Nick, I've heard. Where is everyone?"

The smell of cheap beer was wafting off his breath. "Well, um, I think, I think, uhhh..." I could tell it was taking every brain cell he had to try to form a coherent sentence.

"Never mind," I replied, eager to get away from him, "I'll ask a nurse."

I dashed into the waiting room to find Emily.

Emily was Marie's oldest sister. She was a bit of a drama queen and was always dressed in high-end fashion. It's as if they tore her straight from the pages of Vogue magazine: nose always in the air, eyes rolling at the screech of poor grammar, and the scent of Coco Chanel wafting from her neck. She was a fashion magazine editor, and I found it hard to imagine her in any other world.

In the corner by the soda machine stood Marie's other sisters, Nicole and McKenzie, and hunched over in a chair was her six-foot-five younger brother, Preston. Talk about awkward situations. The silence hung in the air; no one knew what to talk about or whether to talk at all. A nurse came out to speak to the family. "You can go in and see him now," she said.

We slowly walked into the hospital room. There was a somber aura hanging over the room. The hospital lights were dim, the stench of latex and cleaning solution strong.

In the corner stood a tall, thin, doctor with a bald head, holding a clipboard against his white coat. All I could think about was how this man reminded me of a character in a comic I loved, One-Punch Man. He looked just like Saitama, and was just as dry and monotone, jaded in his profession and utterly dispassionate. I barely held in a chuckle at this observation. I fought to hold down the corners of my mouth -- I was always terrible in tragic situations.

But glancing over at Marie's father, lying still in a cold metal bed, my mood shifted. He seemed like a shell of the man I once knew. A machine was breathing for him, and his chest rose and fell with every pump. *This can't be real,* I thought, *How the hell did this happen?* Dave was always in good health, he had some back problems here and there, but he had always been a spry guy, with a dirty mouth straight out of a Tarantino film. But this? This was just soul-crushing.

"We've run several tests," the doctor said.

"And?" Emily snapped.

"Well, so far we are unable to find the source of your father's decline."

"What exactly happened?" I shouted. I paused and immediately clapped my hand over my mouth. My own emotions surprised me, but I had always had a good rapport with Dave. I hated seeing him like this. Maybe it made me think of my own mortality, my kids seeing me in a hospital bed – or worse – one day. I shuddered at the thought.

"He was found in the back office of the shop," Emily said, offering me what little explanation there was, "Barely breathing." Silence struck the room again.

"Can we have a moment alone?" Nicole murmured. The doctor gave a silent nod and vanished into the hallway.

"So, what now?" McKenzie sighed.

"Yeah," Preston replied, "We can't leave him like this."

"I think we all know what must be done." Nicole spoke with a calm, rational tone. *Yeah*, I thought, *pull the plug*. Being in this state forever is not what he would have wanted. "It's time we complete the Three Deeds," Nicole said, putting her hands on her hips and looking over the other siblings. It seemed like she had forgotten I was in the room with them.

"Wait, what three deeds? What is she talking about? Did I miss something Saitama – err, the doctor said?" I looked at Nicole and then at the rest of the siblings. No one would meet my gaze.

"Um, just an old family tradition, like your mother's mac and cheese on Christmas," Marie forced a laugh. "Time to go! " she said, pulling me toward the door. "Why don't we all take some time and I'll talk to the doctor later tonight? We can regroup in the morning."

As she pushed me down the hospital hallway, I could have sworn I saw Uncle Nick sleeping off a hangover in an unused room.

The entire ride to my parents' house to get the kids, I couldn't help but think of what Nicole had said. "Complete the three deeds"? Tradition maybe, but not one that I had ever heard of. What had she been talking about? What exactly had happened to their father?

This bugged me. A lot. It bugged me through dinner, it bugged me through the kids' story time, it bugged me through their bath time, then it bugged me through MY bath time. What did it mean? Before I realized, it was already one in the morning and I had been lying in bed, obsessing. Marie was fast asleep. I couldn't blame her – it had been a long day. Bronx had been snoring on the floor by our bed, but even he was getting tired of listening to me toss and turn. He stood up and padded out of the room, his nails clicking softly in the hallway. Insomnia had sunk its teeth into me with no plans to let go. I gave up and went downstairs to sit on the couch, turning on the TV to take my mind off of things.

By the time I woke up it was three a.m. On the TV, a blonde lady was cheerfully selling vacuums to insomniacs. I found the remote and clicked it off, shrouding the house in darkness. All I could hear was the hum of the fridge in the kitchen. I navigated my house by cell-phone-screen-light and managed to stumble into our bedroom. But something was missing: Marie. I figured she was in the bathroom. Ten minutes went by, and still she didn't appear.

She probably went to the kitchen, I thought, *for a late-night drink.* After all, it had been a stressful day. I turned on my cell phone light, and slowly maneuvered to the kitchen. Empty. Nobody. Maybe she had gone to the bathroom past the kids' basement game room. That was the only place in this house a person could spend five minutes in peace.

Something felt eerie, though.

As I opened the basement door, there was a strange red glow -- a bright red light blistering through the entire game room. *What the hell?* I thought. I cautiously crept down the steps.

What I saw next would change everything.

I crept toward the laundry room; the door was slightly cracked.

I could hear Marie, and at first, I thought she was talking on the phone. But then I began to make out a few other voices -- her brother and sisters. I drew closer, where the red light intensified, and peeked through the cracked wooden door. I forced myself to hold back a gasp. It was Marie. But not *my* Marie.

She had long black hair, with two small golden horns protruding out of her head. Her shoulders bore large regal epaulettes. Her legs were covered in tight black leather leggings with gold and silver plating, and she was in a pair of six-inch black heels. A medallion hung around her neck bearing a large purple gem. A set of black wings bulged out of her back, like the wings of a huge raven. Her stomach was exposed, and only a plate of armor covered her busty chest.

Honestly, it was kind of hot.

What the hell am I thinking, now isn't the time for drooling! What in the world is going on here? I thought, snapping myself back to reality, or the closest thing to it. Her sisters were there as well; their resemblance was similar to Marie's; the only difference was the color of the gem around each of their necks.

Preston, on the other hand, had grown into a hulking beast. I mean, he was always tall, but now he was ponderous. His eyes were a bright amber color. He had massive ram-like horns, armor from head to toe, and he resembled a knight of some kind. At his side he held a great morning star, a large stone ball covered in menacing spikes, attached to a massive chain fit for a tugboat. Behind him swished what looked like a lion's tail. I was frozen, overcome with fear and bewilderment. These people were the ones I called my family. What breed of family was this, exactly?

As McKenzie slowly shifted to one side, I caught a glimpse of a massive floating stone. An artificial voice was floating out of it, saying something about rituals, war, blood ties and the end of an empire. *I can't believe this, no way, it's not real!* I tried to convince myself over and over.

Then it hit me: THE KIDS! I turned around and was prepared to flash up the steps, but that was when I noticed that my steps were not the same – and neither was anything else. The game room wasn't a game room, it resembled that of an old castle dungeon -- a dungeon that still held a slew of my vintage collectibles and games, thank goodness. I must have had half of my net worth wrapped up in those.

What's going on, I wondered. *Is the rest of the house changing, too?*

I backed out of the room as quietly as possible and made my way up the steps to see that the whole house looked like the inside of a castle. As I crept into the kids' room, Harley and Logan were both still sound asleep. At this point, all I could think about was how I was going to get us out of here. No way I was staying in the house with those things, even if one of them was my wife. I figured going out front would be the easiest way out; the back door was far too close to the basement. That's when it hit me: where was Bronx? He could protect us.

I tiptoed down the steps, calling for the dog as quietly as I could manage. "Bronx, psssst! Bronx," I whispered, "Where the hell are you? I bet if I dropped a potato chip, you'd come running." As I got to the third-to-the-last step, my jaw hit the floor. It was Bronx, or at least I thought it was. He lay by the door, practically double in size. And here I thought he was snoring badly before. A puddle of drool laid by his face. *Gross,* I thought, but I wasn't about to try to scold him. He might swallow me whole.

Down Bronx's back was a row of jagged spikes; his teeth were now extra-sharp and overlapped his bottom lip like an alligator's.

Instead of a tail, he had a scaly appendage that twisted and writhed like a snake warming up on hot pavement. *This is like a horror movie,* I thought in a panic. I backpedaled up the steps, soundlessly, back to the kids' room. I had to get my kids out of there. Just as I turned into their room, I caught a whiff of a sweet intoxicating aroma. I had smelled this before…guava? No, honeydew, wait, no… mango! A large puff of smoke appeared, and out of that smoke walked Marie.

"And where do you think you are going?" she said, almost playfully.

I froze in shock. She was coming closer to me, backing me into a wall. Pure fear rained down on me. I was sweating bullets at this point. Before I could blink, Marie thrust her hand out in front of her and my body went limp. She raised her hand to the ceiling and up into the air I went, like a frightened little puppet.

"Oh, you don't have to be afraid, I am your wife after all. For better or worse, right?" she said with a seductive laugh.

This is it, I thought, *I'm dead, so dead,* but I had to do something for my children. That's when I grew a pair.

"Don't hurt my kids!" I shouted.

"Oh baby," said Marie, "Our little monsters are just fine."

I slowly turned my head, and to my dismay and horror, Logan and Harley were up, but it couldn't be them -- no way. I refused to believe my eyes. Logan had horns and a long lion-like tail, and Harley had wings and horns just like Marie. It couldn't be -- my babies, too? Despite their new physical appearance, I had to admit they were still damn cute. Thoughts of my imminent death returned, and I began to sweat again. Marie gestured with her finger for me to come closer, and my body flew over to her.

"What are you gonna do, bite my neck, turn me into a monster, eat me?" I said angrily.

"Oh, I'd *love* to just eat you up. But," she said with a shrug of her shoulders, "The kids are up."

"Well before you kill me, tell me what is going on!" I shouted.

"Kill you?!" Marie chuckled. "Oh sweets, you're far too valuable. But you know our kids. They do love a good bedtime story, so I'll humor you."

I blinked and we were in a green pasture. The air was cool, I could hear birds in the distance. Cattails were whistling in the wind, and I could hear crickets chirring. Dare I say, it was actually beautiful. I glanced over at Harley and Logan, who were chasing each other, round and round in a circle. Despite the madness I was living through that night, I momentarily forgot about it, and felt calm, seeing them so happy. Monsters or not, they were still my little ones. Marie was standing in front of me, gazing at the sunset. She was quiet. At first, I thought to run while she was distracted, but where would I even go?

Stay, I thought, *let me hear what she has to say.* My mouth was dry, my mind was outrunning my words, but I took a deep breath and finally built up the presence of mind to ask her, "What is this? Where are we?" Marie remained silent, unreactive. Staring at her back, it seemed like she was in a different world.

"Marie, so help me, what the hell is this." I was surprised to hear the anger in my own voice. She turned slowly and we locked eyes.

"For better or for worse," she said. "You remember that day, right?" Her eyes began to fill with tears, "Well, this is as bad as it gets."

I looked at the kids and then back at her, and my rage fell away. I took a few steps forward and I put my arms around her. We locked eyes. It felt magnetic, like that night so long ago, on the steps outside of the frat party.

"Empyrean. This is the Empyrean Realm. This is how it begins."

"How what begins?"

Just then I heard a whisper in my mind, *"Your story, love."*

I was perplexed – Marie was in front of me, staring into my eyes, but her lips were not moving. I could hear her whisper in my mind again. *"This is how it came to be."*

And I could see everything: light, dark, and the story of Empyrean.

II
The More You Know

I could hear Marie's voice, telling me a story.

I had always found her voice soothing, and I fell completely under her spell. It was like I was leaving my body, and a great scene opened up before me, a theater in my own mind.

"We've all heard the tale of Angels and Demons, the light and the dark, God versus Lucifer. However, these are the tales of men, and men have a tendency of being counterfactual. The common misconception is that Angels and Demons hate one another and are unable to live harmoniously -- two species interlocked in a good-versus-evil battle for the soul of humanity.

The truth is, they are actually two races that shared the same world, one called The Empyrean Realm, a great city in the nexus of everything that is. Although the two species coexisted, they couldn't be more different.

The Angels were a regal race, elegant, and vibrant. They enjoyed finery, leisure, and pleasure, preferring to outsource physical labor in order to focus on pursuits of the mind. Angels excelled at technological advancements.

Angels used halos to enhance their ability to manifest magic and interstellar energy into a tangible force. The most powerful Angels could generate enough interstellar energy to rival that of a supernova. Over time the Angels found ways to use this ability to make great strides in the sciences.

The wings of an Angel were massive and opulent. Angels used their wings as a sign of wealth and class. The bigger and more beautiful, the more important the Angel was. Upon first glance, they appeared delicate. But Angel wings were as sharp as blades and hard as the finest metals.

The Demons were a warrior and builder race. Unrestrained, exuberant, and carefree, they were capable of building the most beautiful architecture and weapons.

When men hear the word "Demon" they think of the stuff of nightmares, and they wouldn't be wrong to do so. Male Demons were often large and intimidating. They possessed tails similar to that of an earth lion and had massive horns, but they did not have wings. What they lacked in wings, however, they made up for with their immense strength. Male Demons played the role of guardian and protector within their families. Typically, they left decision-making to the females, as they tended to be more rational than the males.

Female Demons' strength lay in magic and incantations, using both as a means of getting what they desired from their male counterparts. The females were known for their flirtatious and seductive natures. They were often the leaders and controllers of their houses. They possessed smaller horns and no tail but had black bird-like wings. Though not as physically powerful as their male counterparts, a female Demon's speed was unmatched.

Both Angels and Demons were scanned for their level of power at the time of their birth, and ranked in class, from A through F. Most of the Empyrean population ranked D-class, but because there is no society without corruption, not even one made up of Angels and Demons, those who had the means to do so would sometimes bribe the voices in power for a slightly higher distinction. But it was impossible to bribe one's way into A-class, as those in the A-class were unrivaled in their strength and intellect, traits that were hard to feign. While the Angels excelled in science and technology, Demons mastered the art of craftsmanship, mining, and building. Every Demon possessed the ability to use telekinesis and magic, which made mining metals and Empyrean ore exceedingly simple. Rumor had it, the greatest Demons were capable of lifting stones the size of a moon. The two races used their complementary strengths to build a Utopia. The Demons crafted the framework of the city while the Angels developed cutting-edge technology. This relationship and bond were integrated into everything. Demons knew of the Angels' taste for beauty and aesthetics, so they would build sumptuous armor encrusted with precious jewels, smelting weapons fit for a god. The Angels would then infuse these items with technology that would enhance the wearer's speed, strength, and dexterity. In return, the Angels provided the use of technology throughout the city, making all aspects of daily life comfortable and efficient.

There was virtually nothing to fear within the grand city. However, there was one thing that would attack an Angel or Demon: the Grootslang. Massive serpent-like monsters with tusks, the Grootslang were creatures believed to be older than space and time. A failed attempt at perfection by the Gods of Old, Grootslang came before both the Angel and Demon races. The Grootslang had only one desire, to absorb light and dark energy. They were primitive creatures with no rationale or reason who often lingered on the outskirts of Empyrean, notorious for feasting on Angels and Demons, often attacking the great city to satiate their appetites. Araqiel repeatedly sent troops to deal with the beasts, but few lived to tell the tale of the encounter. To protect his citizens and avoid more casualties, King Araqiel had a great wall built around Empyrean that completely cut the Grootslang off. Only a fool would venture past its haven.

Aside from the Grootslang, Empyrean was perfect under the watchful eye of King Araqiel, the strongest of the Angels. Under his ordinance Empyrean was truly bliss. Like any effective ruler, King Araqiel concerned himself with not only the people of the kingdom but his public image. Empyrean inhabitants had always viewed his choices as fair and just. Araqiel truly believed in the harmony of Angel- and Demon-kind. But even though he was the supreme ruler, all decisions went through the Grand Synod, and not everyone there shared his passion for fellowship.

The only Angel in the Kingdom of Empyrean that came close to matching King Araqiel's sheer strength was Loath. He had a seat on the Grand Synod and had trouble hiding his distaste for Demons. He was a tall, thin Angel, with short blonde hair: no other Angel in all of Empyrean rivaled Loath's fairness, no female could bask in his glory, no male but the king himself and the Demon Camio could test his talents in combat. Loath was an expert swordsman, known for his skill and dexterity with a blade. Such talent and potential were countered only by his lust for unchecked power.

There were Demons on the Synod that detested Angels in much the same way. Chief among them was the Demon Camio, the Field Marshal of the Empyrean Empire. He was Araqiel's right hand, with a sharp intellect and enviable physical strength. Camio's love for Demon-kind was no secret, but he concealed a deep hatred for Angels. However, Camio, unlike Loath, was clever enough to disguise his ardent partisanship. Loath knew of Camio's true feelings, but it would have been unwise to challenge Camio -- his bloodline was rumored to be one of the most powerful in Empyrean.

In Loath's eyes, the alliance between Araqiel and Camio was a true abomination. Moreover, events to come would continue to test

Loath's faith in Araqiel's leadership.

It was under Araqiel's direction that the scientist known as Pronoia would soon make great technological leaps with the project code-named "Transient". Araqiel believed that the next step in evolution was seeded in artificially created life: living beings intertwined with technology. This lifeform could learn and grow with minimal guidance. It would be named "Project Transient." Transients were designed to serve and live among their benevolent masters, the Angels and Demons. They were capable of learning but showed virtually no emotions, due to the lack of a soul.

Loath was horrified and disgusted at the prospect of a King, an Angel of the highest caliber, investing so much time in unworthy beings: first Demons, now puppets. He could not stand by silently any longer. His pride was a dangerous venom, and he was its unwitting victim.

Free speech is a right inextricable from its consequences, a lesson Loath would soon learn. He spoke out about his feelings to the council, believing that they catered to beasts and marionettes, that the king had a foolish vision, and that the Angels were the true masters. Loath believed that the angels were driven and hard-working, unlike the slothful Demons, thus making the Angels closer to the Gods of Old -- the true embodiment of perfection, cured over time.

You see, the Gods of Old are believed to be the creators of the Angels and Demons, but grew weary of meddling in their affairs, trusting the races to resolve their issues of their own volition. The idea of proving one's competence to the Old Gods was viewed as one way of walking in their image.

For his impertinence, Loath was removed from the council. Loath found King Araqiel and The Synod's decision unconscionable. How could he be removed while an animal like Camio roamed free, unchecked within the castle walls?

Loath decided they would pay, and the kingdom would suffer for its disrespect. Pride and rage are easy motivators, and Loath took his rage out on the symbol of his contempt: a small Demon village. In one night, Loath decimated the entire population of that Demon settlement. Even the youngest Demons would meet their demise at the point of his blade. The few that survived would never fully recover from their wounds. Word of this genocide did not take long to reach Araqiel, who was devastated and bewildered. An Angel, a being of light, was committing terrible crimes.

Araqiel enlisted his personal guard, the Knights of Sistine Madonna, to bring Loath to justice. They were three Angels and three Demons, five of them ranked as B-class.

The leader of this group, Daevas, was an A-class Demon, the same rank as Loath, Camio, and King Araqiel himself. The Knights began their hunt for the once-honored Angel, now a fugitive with blood on his hands. It did not take long for Daevas and his men to find Loath. He was strong, but no match for the combined efforts of the Knights.

The two cardinal rules of Empyrean are simple. First, "Integration without consent is viewed as an abomination." Angels and Demons may share a world, but blood is to remain pure. Within the dark markets of Empyrean, Angel and Demon blood was sold as a delicacy. Some of the elder Angels and Demons believed that ingesting the blood of the opposite race would give one hybrid-like abilities, as well as enhanced insight into the others' world. Of course, these were no more than old wive's tales. Those who were caught indulging in such faced immediate and total banishment to the Outskirts.

However, "Thou shall not kill" was a law that surpassed the former in gravity. The Grand Synod would not be forgiving toward Loath. In the entire history of Empyrean's existence, no soul had committed a single murder until now.

Moreover, politics played a role in the king's handling of Loath's crime. If word ever spread that an Angel was responsible for what men understand as a hate-crime, it could lead to civil war. The Synod as well as the rest of Empyrean's inhabitants must never find out. They would certainly demand execution of Loath for these murders, and Demon riots would ensue, thus bringing chaos to the kingdom. Araqiel's name, and his rule, would be irrevocably tarnished.

Racked by fear and indecision, Araqiel consulted with his right hand, Camio. The cunning Camio convinced Araqiel that executing Loath was not nearly as harsh as banishment. Banishment could easily be disguised as a sort of pilgrimage. The slaying of a Demon village could be blamed on the Grootslang – this would be not be difficult for Empyrean's citizens to believe. The king's image was to be protected, and civil war avoided at all costs.

For his crimes, Loath was sentenced to eternity in Damabiath, a prison in the deepest regions of the universe, a land of brimstone and pure darkness.

But upon Loath's arrival to the prison, Camio was there waiting for him.

Like Loath, Camio believed that his race was superior in every way. He also felt that the Angels had been using Demons for far too long. Camio wanted the kingdom divided, with Demons on one side and Angels on the other. He proposed his plan to Loath. He would give Araqiel's Transients the one thing they lacked: a soul. Camio was not a scientist, but he was self-taught in the art of Transient soul infusion. Camio believed that once given souls, he could convince Transients to question why Araqiel would leave out such an essential part of their programming. Why would he not want them to have the same rights? Camio knew this would cause the Transients to revolt.

The first of the Transients that would be given the glory of a soul by Camio would be named Merozantine. Merozantine had been a personal servant to Loath, who had not supported the Transient project, but did not refrain from exploiting their servitude. Now that Merozantine was without a master, he would be the perfect subject to receive a soul.

Camio knew that once Merozantine learned of the banishment of his master, and the fact that Araqiel had withheld souls from the Transients, he would be more than willing to lead a revolt. Anger needs time to take hold and fester, so Camio promised Merozantine a world of his own, where he and other Transients could form their own kingdom. This plane would be known as Terra. With the use of interstellar Angel technology, Camio transported Merozantine and his group to Terra. He showed Merozantine and his people how to build a kingdom and grow as a civilization. On the heels of this knowledge came the birth of greed, power, and lust.

The grateful Merozantine was given a blade called The Sword of Grus. It could open a direct link to Camio himself. But with this contraband came a curse, capable of infecting Angels and Demons.

Camio told Merozantine that he would return in three Terra-centuries, the equivalent of three Empyrean weeks. This would give Merozantine and his people the time they needed to create an army. With Camio's knowledge of the kingdom's layout he would then smuggle Merozantine and his men into the castle. Once inside, they could ambush the King and demand a seat within the Empyrean realm, basking in the rays of eternal life.

As the centuries passed, and the Merozantine civilization grew into a kingdom, it would branch off into different fractions, producing various other races, each with their own kingdoms across Terra. Nevertheless, the Merozantine Empire remained the largest.

Merozantine's bloodline would flow through the ages.

The centuries had ticked down to the day that Camio would return to lead his army. The sword began to glow, its power causing the earth to shake, the ocean to spew forth tidal waves, and the sky to turn black as the darkest corners of space.

It was time for King Merozantine VI to fulfill the destiny of his fathers before him and restore the Transients to their rightful place in the Kingdom of Empyrean, not as servants but as equals. A great portal opened before King Merozantine VI and his militia. Camio arrived in a grand chariot loaded with the highest-quality Demon weapons and armor fitted with Angel technology.

King Merozantine VI withdrew Grus from the scabbard at his side and presented the great blade to Camio, pledging not just his loyalty, but that of the entire Merozantine bloodline. Camio drew his saber, the mighty Byzantine, a weapon very seldom removed from its sheath. He crossed blades with Grus, and at once Merozantine and his troops were engulfed in smoke and transported to the Grand Empyrean Castle.

The great invasion began. It was an attack so brutal that it would later be referred to as the Temptation Raid. Merozantine and his troops slaughtered Angels and Demons within the castle, sparing no one. The armor and weapons given to Merozantine troops were beyond powerful, and Araqiel's men were unprepared for such an audacious and well-equipped onslaught. Merozantine's rage was unmatched and unbridled.

Merozantine VI did not know it, but he had been enchanted, and was under Camio's control. What a pity, to end up entirely in the thrall of the man who had given him a soul capable of free will.

With the castle under siege, Araqiel sent for Daevas and the Knights of the Sistine Madonna. He was confident the Knights could handle Merozantine's forces within the Castle.

Daevas and the Knights arrived quickly, and immediately sensed trouble when they saw the rogue Transient army. The armor they had donned, it was certainly Demon- and Angel-crafted, but the crest on the armor -- it was the crest of the Ashi! This was the crest worn only by Daevas' family line, the Ashi; and the Knights of the Sistine Madonna. How could it be that these Transients were wearing it? Frozen with puzzlement, Daevas reacted to the confusion by momentarily halting the knights' assault. Araqiel, upon seeing the armor, assumed there was treachery within his kingdom – this army was made of Empyrean traitors. Camio had painted a false picture for the king's eyes. The king gathered that the rogue Transients aligned themselves with Daevas, bearing his crest and seeking power. This lie poisoned Araqiel's trust in Deavas and his Knights.

King Merozantine himself, even under Camio's enchantment, vaguely suspected something was wrong upon seeing the crest. *Why would Camio blend us in so well with the enemy?* He wondered. Yet before King Merozantine could speak, he was stabbed in the back by Camio, silenced permanently. Daevas, being a sharp judge of character, suspected Camio's treachery and pleaded with Araqiel to see through the charade. However, Camio's charm was stronger than Daevas' suspicion. Araqiel believed his most trusted right hand.

Empyrean reinforcements arrived, and under Araqiel's command, slew Merozantine's troops.

Meanwhile, the Synod, unaware of the chaos breaking out within the eastern regions of the castle, had suddenly to contend with a surprise visitor. A disheveled Loath burst through the grand council doors, interrupting their session. The Angel banished to the dark region of Damabiath had returned. Loath, blessed with the gift of a silver tongue, convinced the Synod that it was Araqiel's precious

Transients that had slain the innocent Demon families that unfortunate night. Carefully orchestrating the plot Camio had devised with him during his time in banishment, Loath explained to the Synod that Araqiel and Daevas knew of this, and though Loath had often expressed his dislike of Demons, he would never wish death upon them. Loath suggested that Araqiel and Daevas had banished him to Damabiath as a tactic to silence him. His conviction was so seamless that he convinced the Synod to take action against Araqiel.

With all the lies in place -- a king accusing his greatest Knights, a council accusing its king -- punishments were meted out. The Synod, in times of war, reserved the right to strip any king of his crown if the situation necessitated. What more fitting punishment for abusing his power and covering up a genocide than to banish Araqiel to Damabiath?

As for Daevas, some considered his punishment to be far worse. For crimes against the kingdom, Daevas was charged with conspiracy. He was sentenced to undergo the Dark Mutatio, a curse infused with ancient Demonic magic, a curse only Pronoia, the creator of the Transients, could successfully conjure. Such a curse extracted the very soul of Daevas and trapped it in a Transient shell, banishing it to Terra.

Camio would go to even greater lengths to make sure this curse would never be lifted. He applied three ancient Demon talismans to the cursed Transient, which could only be broken when the Three Deeds had been fulfilled.

First, one of Daevas' children must wed into the family of the Merozantine;

Once wed into the Merozantine bloodline, a seed must be spawned; and finally,

The Sword of Grus must be returned to the rightful king of the

Merozantine Empire.

Camio ordered the remaining Merozantine Empire to be eradicated by a new superweapon, The Durendal Cannon. It was the greatest weapon ever created through Demon mechanization and Angel technology. A weapon crafted without Araqiel's knowledge; it was powered by harvested Grootslang souls. The Durendal Cannon could wipe out a kingdom in a single blast. Thus, the Merozantine bloodline was wiped from existence, relegated to a fragment of memory.

As for the Knights of the Sistine Madonna, Camio ordered Pronoia to cast another spell. This spell would transform the knights into truly vicious beings that he renamed the Beasts of the Madonna. These six great beasts were given the task of guarding the cell of Araqiel on Damabiath. They also kept the the Sword of Grus from ever seeing the light of day, hidden in a secret chamber deep beneath Empyrean inside a series of labyrinths. Only a fool would dare to infiltrate, for three of the beasts protected the sword, and three protected the access points leading to Araqiel's cell suspended in the air deep within the labyrinth, a true hell for any trespassers.

Each Beast was endowed with extreme powers: Catacomb, of the darkness, a cunning Demon who possessed the ability to invade dreams; Flower, of the poison, a Demon who used magic to manipulate organic plant life; Herculean, of the power, an Angel whose body size had been enhanced with technology and was now more machine than Angel; Torrid, of the flame, a Demon with complete mastery over Fire; Wolf, of the sheep, an Angel who had the ability to absorb powers and use them as her own; and Meridian, of the chrónos, an Angel with the ability to control portions of time. To ensure their subservience, they were reined by a spell to obey the wills of their new masters, Camio and Loath.

With the close of the Era of Araqiel, the Empyrean Empire was heading into a dark age. Only a new and just ruler could restore Empyrean to its former bliss, a brilliant jewel in a dim universe.

With the deposing of Araqiel, the throne hung like a low-hanging fruit, ripe for picking. Camio and Loath convinced the Synod that the wisest course of action would be to divide Empyrean. With the political upheavals and wanton killings fresh in the minds of the people, the last thing the Synod needed was a civil war between Angels and Demons. The council reluctantly agreed to the division. Empyrean would be split into two separate kingdoms, Camio and Loath each the respective keeper of his race.

To the north of Empyrean would be Dada, Province of the Angels, and to the South lay Gauguin, House of the Demons.

Not all were pleased with this fissure, so a third plane was created in secrecy. A town plagued with scoundrels and rogues; this was home to those who did not believe in the Empyrean's sectarian kings. It was a haven for poverty and theft: The Aisle of Oldenburg.

Oldenburg held its secrets close to its chest. In this town dwelled the family of disgraced Demon Daevas. After their father's banishment, the five children retreated to Oldenberg, governing the lawless town while endlessly seeking a way to restore their father to his former greatness. Together they would try to expose the lies of Camio and Loath and bring justice back to Empyrean. Using a sophisticated underground network of spies, and where necessary, mercenaries, the siblings discovered the way to restore Daevas from his Transient form. It would not be easy, but anything worth fighting for usually isn't. Through their information channels, the siblings had discovered the Three Deeds set in place by Camio.

This would be no simple mission, for their first task was to steal the Sword of Grus. This proved to be a dangerous endeavor. The siblings were successful in retrieving the great sword from within the underground labyrinths beneath Empyrean. During the retrieval, the Beasts of the Madonna ambushed the siblings and a fearsome battle broke out. Efforts were made to wield the sword, but as Daevas' children discovered, outside of King Merozantine's hands it was but a mere blade. This battle was so fierce that the sword was broken into four pieces. In a desperate effort to keep the pieces out of the clutches of the Madonna, Marie summoned a portal of dark magic to transport the broken sword to the realm known as Terra. The siblings were no match for the powerful Beast of the Madonna and decided it would be best to retreat through the dark portal, following the broken sword. However, during the leap through realms, the pieces were scattered and lost on Terra. With their reserves of Dark magic now expended, the siblings found themselves stranded there until their father's power was restored.

Destiny finds us all, they say. Little did Camio and Loath know, even they couldn't run from fate. Centuries had passed and a battle was brewing.

A bright flash flooded my mind's eye, leaving me disoriented. I felt as if I had woken from a vivid dream.

"Where am I, am I back in my body? Marie, what was all of that? What did I just see?"

She stood there silently, sadness written across her face.

"Marie! Answer me!" I said. «Gosh, I might as well be talking to Bronx."

I started to think about the vision I just experienced. It felt horrible, but what did any of it have to do with me?

Marie laughed mirthlessly. Tears poured down her face as she laughed. I couldn't understand what she was feeling, and her mood was beginning to worry me.

Oh Tyler, you have no idea, Marie's voice echoed in my skull.

How does she keep getting inside my head? I guess this explains how she always knows when I'm lying.

"Oh, sweets," she cackled. "You've always been slow on the draw. Typical Merozantine."

"Wait, Merozantine?!" I cried, "You mean...?" My face turned as pale as a china doll's face. I felt my stomach churning, round and round like a cement truck.

It can't be! I thought wildly.

"God, baby, get a clue; Pine isn't your surname."

It couldn't be true. But even as I denied her words, the vivid images I had just been shown haunted me. I knew she had to be telling the truth. I could feel it in my bones.

III
Mondays

A week had passed since my first vision and I still had so many questions.

It turns out we were never really on Empyrean; it was all dark magic that Marie had concocted to show me her true home. It all felt so real, though. I asked Marie why our house had changed in appearance that night. Well, it turns out that the house we live in is actually a castle that's camouflaged to look like an ordinary house. Marie and her siblings had it built as a base of sorts over 400 years ago. And as you may have already guessed, 400 years is nothing for a Demon.

Marie and her family have been on earth (or Terra, as they call it) for centuries. They disguised themselves to fit in – human appearance, regular clothes, normal middle-class-looking homes, steady jobs. But let's talk about the most ridiculous part of all of this: I'm a descendant of this Merozantine guy! To be fair, I don't doubt that Marie is right. She knows her stuff. I guess when you've been alive as long as her, you learn a thing or two. And to think, I've seen her go ballistic over a lone gray hair.

So, how did my line survive, anyway? By all appearances, that Camio guy's superweapon had wiped my ancestors from existence. As fate would have it, when Camio blew up the Merozantine Empire, he didn't count on King Merozantine VI being a bit of a sleaze-ball, who slept around behind his wife's back. That's right: the king had a child out of wedlock, and that's the guy who turned out to be my great, great, great, great ancestor.

As Marie revealed more and more to me over the next few days, I found that I was just as big a piece to this puzzle as they were. Marie told me, once I had a little time to recover from the shock, "You, Tyler, are the only person that can wield the Sword of Grus."

Quite honestly, I didn't really want to wield anything. I don't know how to fight Demons or Angels, and I'm definitely not meant to be some heir to anyone's throne.

* * *

"Tyler, Tyler!"

God, I would have known that nasal voice anywhere. It was Natalie White. It seemed I was past due for my monthly ball-busting. Gotta love Mondays. "Tyler, did you get a chance to look over the document I've emailed you?" Natalie said in her usual condescending tone.

Right; let me get on that, I thought. Not like I'm in the middle of an ancient war or anything! If only I had the courage to be so blunt. "Sure did, Natalie," I happily groveled. Wow. So long, spine.

This was going to be a long day. I looked at the clock on my computer monitor, and the minutes started to seem like hours. Eventually, after what seemed like an eon, it was noon. My coworkers drifted to the lunchroom. I have always preferred to eat alone. Plus, being on my own gives me time to think. It was spookily quiet in the office as I ate my sandwich and let my mind wander. The quiet hum of my computer fan fell in tempo with my heart rate. Gradually, I began to notice my vision getting cloudier. Then I realized it wasn't my vision, it was purple smoke rising around me until I couldn't even see my hands in front of me.

"Oh no...," I groaned, watching the office walls around me dissipate. Before I could blink, I was back in my house – or, I guess, castle. Marie floated above me, as though perched on an invisible cushion. All I could think was, Man, this demon is hot, could she stay in this form permanently? But never mind that. She had already started to talk, and I hadn't heard a word of it.

"What now, Marie? I have work to do. And speaking of work, why aren't you there?"

"Oh, sweets; temper, temper. Maybe if you checked the kitchen calendar once in a while, you'd know this is my day off!" Marie responded with a grin. "Anyway, I brought you back here because all this time we haven't been able to locate a single piece of that sword. But since you've been informed of your lineage, Preston has been able to detect vast amounts of energy in various regions on Terra."

"Okay, what's your point?" I replied. No matter how much I learned from Marie and her siblings, it felt like I could never keep up, a fact that was becoming deeply frustrating.

Marie snapped her fingers and my body lifted off the floor and flew up until we were face to face. "What it means is, the time is now! We must form the sword so you can use it!" shouted Marie.

I really had to get used to this sudden floating-off-the-ground-and-being-shouted-at stuff. "In case you forgot, Marie, I'M A HUMAN! I'm useless to your cause."

Marie let out a laugh. "You don't listen very well, do you? In order to get father out of that dying Transient body, we must complete the Three Deeds. This is the last deed, and you're a Merozantine. You are very important!"

Marie lowered her chin and looked up at me through her eyelashes with a piteous expression. Her lower lip jutted ever so slightly. She's always been good at pulling my heartstrings. "Tyler, we need that sword. But as I'm sure you can guess, we're not the only ones looking for the pieces. I'm sure Camio has already sent the Madonna, and I fear the worst."

Hm, the Madonna. If these guys are as strong as they say they are, then there really is no hope for Marie and her siblings. I can't just let her family -- my family -- go through this.

I set my jaw.

"Okay Marie, tell me what I need to do." I could feel my blood pressure rising. I was hyped for sure. That, or I'm about to have a heart attack, I thought. Nope, pretty sure this is anger. "Camio, Loath, and the rest of these jerks will pay. We will end this, I promise!"

Marie looked at me and grabbed my shirt, pulling me closer, locking me into a kiss. It was so hot. I felt like a nerdy high school kid living out his wildest fantasy. I mean, who knew I would be making out with a real Demon one day?

"Good to know where you stand," Marie said, breaking away from my lips. "Now, we train you to hunt Angels and Demons." In seconds, Marie was back in her human form. "Well, time to take Logan to Toddler Time at the Library," she said with a sweet smile. "Toodles!"

Marie wasn't joking when she said I'd be training hard. My days were spent being a dad, a depressed employee, and a husband. My nights, however, were spent in what my Demon in-laws called the Usugurai.

The Usugurai is a dream realm city. The only way to get to the Usugurai is to have a lucid dream, something that Marie had begun teaching me to do every night – although, to be honest, it wasn't hard to fall into a deep sleep after a full day of working, being a dad, and absorbing all the Demon knowledge being crammed into me every day.

I met Preston at the entrance to the city. Together, we trekked through the Usugurai. On the way, Preston explained to me that we were heading toward the Beach of Acheron, which I could only enter by eating a special seed. "This is called the Limbic Seed," he said, reaching his huge paw-like hand toward mine and placing a small black seed into my palm. "Don't lose it!" he said, with the same slightly parental edge in his voice that Marie got when she was telling me to pay attention or ordering me to do a chore. I rolled my eyes but made sure to place the seed carefully into my pocket. After a time that felt like an hour but could have been mere seconds, we reached a vast body of black water.

"This is it," said Preston. "Time to eat up." He casually threw a seed into his mouth.

I removed the seed from my pocket, and quickly swallowed it. It reminded me of a raw pumpkin seed, chewy and kind of bitter but not terrible. The effects, however, were fast and unrelenting. I had always been a total square and never did any sort of drug, but this feeling -- it was like every cliché you've ever heard about drugs, multiplied by twenty. Colors were intense and vivid and vibrated in the air, emitting their own sounds. I felt so light, like I could float away any second. My pupils swelled to the size of black marbles and every hair on my body danced. It actually kind of tickled. As my body grew accustomed to the strange new feelings, the sensations quieted down into a low hum, like a hive of bumblebees hibernating in my belly. Gradually, I could see a long brick path taking shape in front of me, arcing over the black body of water. I understood now that this seed was helping me see what had been there, all along. This was our way to the Beach of Acheron. I followed Preston as he stepped onto the path, the black water churning beneath us.

Preston explained that Acheron is where some of the strongest dark creatures take shape; they're also known, unsurprisingly, as Nightmares. Whenever you have a nightmare that seems real, it more than likely formed in the Beach of Acheron, made its way to Usugurai, and found you in your dream-state. Think of Usugurai as a world with its own little hell -- Acheron.

For years, this practice of sparring in Usugurai was used by Angels and Demons to hone their skills without losing their life force. Not many humans go because they can't handle it. Marie told me I was different, because of my lineage. Preston claimed that if I could learn to fight on the Beach of Acheron, I'd eventually be able to use those skills on Terra. I had to admit, this was all starting to sound so cool.

Preston and I both arrived on the Beach of Acheron, and let's just say, it was no Praia do Rosa. The sand was the color of ash, as if a volcano erupted upon it. Steam from the black waters added to the stagnant fog as it rolled across the beach, coming up to my knees. It was as if a Halloween fog machine were running on the beach. I've always hated Halloween. It's too scary for my taste. Goblins, killer clowns, strangers giving out candy -- no thanks. Besides, when I was younger the neighborhood kids would play horrible pranks on me. Once it was so bad, I even wet myself.

I slowly walked over to where the water was lapping the shore and picked up what looked like a clamshell the size of my shoe, only to have a gross tentacle slither out from between its halves. I immediately tossed the shell back into the murky waters. My inner chicken was flaring up again. This was definitely not my kind of beach.

"If you're going to be in this war, it's time you learned how to use a blade," Preston said. He gestured for me to pick up a blade on the sand next to him and was already removing his from its scabbard.

Preston showed me how to hold a sword, how to thrust, to counter a blow, how to fake out my opponent, and how to deliver speed and power in one movement. It was the hardest workout I had ever undertaken, and there was still so much to learn, so much to practice. In between sparring matches, I asked Preston more questions. My mind was open now, and where I had been overwhelmed with information as I fell into sleep, I now felt mentally refreshed and ready to hear more. I wondered if it was the physical workout I was getting, the effect of the Limbic Seed, the strange dream-world taking its hold on me, or a combination of all three.

"This sword fighting has got me wondering: why didn't this Camio guy just destroy the Sword of Grus?"

"When a weapon is forged," Preston explained, "It is forged to match the exact attributes of its wielder. For example, Camio is an A-class Demon, and so is the Sword of Grus. The only way for someone to wield a weapon of higher caliber is to have it bestowed upon them. However, in that process, the owner relinquishes all rights to the weapon, even the ability to destroy it. At best the weapon could be fractured, the way Grus was broken into shards. When Camio bestowed Grus upon Merozantine, he gave up the right to destroy the weapon. So as powerful as Camio is, he could do nothing with the sword but fight with it as though it was a mere blade, leaving it exposed to potential damage. Camio is smart: he wouldn't risk wielding the weapon, potentially allowing it in the hands of those who were in favor of reviving Daevas." He paused.

"Then you came into the picture."

We trained for what felt like hours. Preston in his Demon form was immensely strong. While I rested between our sparring matches, he demonstrated moves for me using his sword and his morning star. His fighting ability was incredible. It was like witnessing a violent ballet. In one swing, he was able to slay ten Nightmares, and to him it was simply a warm-up. Meanwhile, there I was, practically peeing my pants at the sight of the terrible creatures.

"So, Preston," I asked quietly, "We can't die here, can we?"

Preston let out a grand laugh. "Well, I can't," he bellowed. "But humans that venture here usually end up in Oblivion."

"What the hell is Oblivion?" I croaked.

"Ever hear of a coma?"

Okay, so I needed to figure this out fast. This wasn't like a videogame, where there were two more lives waiting for me in the corner. I drew the blade Preston gave me. My legs felt like they would give out under me at any moment. A giant hound-like creature crept from out of the fog, gnashing his teeth as he slowly approached me.

"Wait, wait, wait, Preston. What the heck is that thing?!" I stuttered.

"That, Tyler, is another Nightmare. They mostly take the shape of one's fears."

That explained it. I had always been afraid of dogs. When I was six, I was chased down my street by my neighbor's black Doberman and forced to take refuge on top of an old van. It wasn't until I met Marie's dog, Bronx, that I learned to love dogs. But I clearly still had some lingering fears, by the looks of this Nightmare. As it ambled closer to me it looked more and more like that dog from my childhood -- if that dog had injected steroids and pumped iron every day.

"Steady, Tyler," Preston said in a low voice, "Nightmares are relatively weak, but for a beginner, I suggest caution."

The hound inched closer toward me, long strings of saliva hanging from his lips. I wished I could assure the beast that my scrawny body had no flavor. "I'm practically skin and bone," I pleaded as he let out a low growl. I cautiously backed away. Preston stood off to the side with his huge arms crossed over his barrel chest. He's not going to help me -- is he serious?

"Focus!" Preston shouted. "Look closely at the nightmare and remember you're a Merozantine. Ancient Empyrean programming courses through your veins! If you focus hard enough, you can see as the ancient Merozantine have."

I had no idea what he meant, but I decided to trust his word. With a deep breath, I closed my eyes, and I felt my world slowing down. It was weird -- I could feel the Nightmare breathing and its heart beating as though its organs were inside of me. I opened my eyes, and the Nightmare was now emitting a bright hot yellow aura. And something was different: a single spot just above his right paw was glowing purple.

"NOW, TYLER!" Preston shouted. The Nightmare lunged toward me, I stepped back on my left foot and lashed out my blade with everything I had. The Nightmare's dismembered paw flew into the air as it let out a great howl.

"Don't let up Tyler, finish him," Preston shouted.

The beast was weakened, but still functioning on three legs. He still had some fight left. Still able to run, the hound lunged at my face, and I leaned back as if I were Neo in The Matrix, jabbing my blade through the belly of the beast. It howled out a final cry and turned into ashes.

For a moment, I stood there pouring sweat. My mouth was as dry as the beach and I was covered in black sand from head to toe. I could feel the dense fog taking up real estate inside my lungs. I fell face first into the black sand and lay there for a moment, catching my breath. Then, in stunned silence, I sat up to stare at the space where the Nightmare had once stood. I let out an adrenaline-fueled whoop.

"What? How? Preston, what was that?!"

Preston chuckled. "That, Tyler, is called Próvlepsi. It's a technique that the ancient Transients were given. They initially used it to detect injuries. During combat with, say, a Grootslang, Demons and Angels would require treatment. Transients would sometimes act as field nurses, and scan for the injuries so healing magic could be administered. You can use this ability to find old injuries, areas of weakness, and use them as points of attack."

"Man, I'm beat; can we call it quits for today?"

"Before we go back, I'd like to give you something," said Preston.

A gift? This guy is full of surprises, I thought. Preston stood looming in front of me, my head coming to about his navel.

"Take this." He stretched out his massive hand and gave me what appeared to be a toothbrush.

"What exactly are you saying, Preston? Does my breath smell that bad?"

Preston shook his head and sighed. "It's called a disguise, Tyler. Concentrate, and it will take its true form!"

God, you'd think a few centuries on earth would make a person better at understanding what a good disguise is, I thought. But never mind that. It was time to see what this baby could do. I held the toothbrush in my right hand. I closed my eyes and focused. Everything seemed to slow down, like when I was facing off with the Nightmare. My palm grew warm. Then I experienced a surge of energy. My body began to glow a hot red, and before my eyes, the toothbrush transformed. Before I knew it, it had become a sword! It was incredible to see.

"This is the Sardna," Preston said. "It's not nearly as powerful as Grus. But it will surely help you fend off anything Camio and Loath send your way."

"What about the Madonna?" I hastened to ask.

Preston sighed heavily. "Unfortunately, I don't think this will be enough for the Madonna. If you encounter any of them, you promise me one thing."

"And that is?"

Preston put his hulking hand on my boney shoulder and dropped to one knee so that he could look into my eyes. "Run."

"What if a piece of the sword is near?" I replied.

"Even so," said Preston.

I lowered my head in defeat, acutely aware that I needed to get stronger somehow. I just needed time. Speaking of which, yikes! I had to get ready for work shortly. I whipped my head around, looking for an exit sign.

Preston began to chuckle, "What are you doing, Tyler?"

"I have to go to work, I've been here for hours," I started frantically, "Natalie is going to eat my soul if I'm late…"

"You can relax. Here in Usugurai, time moves differently. Five hours here is only a few minutes in the real world. At worst, it's one in the morning on Terra."

The next morning at work was brutal. I couldn't focus on any of my tasks. Not to mention I was beat. Even though the training took place in a dream realm, my body was sore as though it had all happened in my waking life. I figured an outdoor stroll would refresh me. As I gingerly paced down the campus steps, I spotted Justin outside. I had to admit, I hadn't been the greatest friend as of late. But how could I be? I mean Demons, really? It was almost too much just to maintain the responsibilities I had at home on any given day, let alone nurture my withering friendships. I tried to slip away unnoticed.

"Tyler! Yo, Ty!" he shouted.

Oh crap, too late, I've been spotted.

"Oh hey...Justin, what's up? Long time, no see," I feigned enthusiasm. "What brings you to campus?"

Justin adjusted the strap of his messenger bag and began to fix his tie, which had been draped loosely around his neck. I noticed it was patterned with little yellow rubber ducks.

"Got myself an interview, bro! Assistant fitness instructor. I sent you a text about it, remember?"

"Yeah... a text, definitely." We stood there for a moment, an awkward silence hanging between us. I could tell Justin wanted to say more. He looked so...well, vulnerable, if a guy can say that about his bro. I wondered if he saw the guilt in my eyes. "Anyway, hey, good luck," I said, struggling to smile.

I wanted to say so much more, but I couldn't just spring all this demon stuff on him. And besides, would he even believe me? Best friend or not, my life was teetering on insane.

Justin glanced at his cell phone. "Well, I gotta dip out. But if I get this gig, maybe we can go celebrate, bro."

"For sure," I called as he dashed into the building.

I continued my walk around the campus, thinking about that saying, "Friends come into your life for a reason, a season, or a lifetime." It was one of those stupid clichés that people loved to post on their social media, but I had never really given it any serious consideration. I wondered what category Justin fell into. Hell, I wondered what category I fell into for him. I made a promise to myself that I wouldn't be a crappy friend anymore. But I needed to figure out how to help Marie's family first.

As I walked around, musing over everything, I began to feel that I was being watched. The hairs on my neck would often stand up, but I would look around me and nothing appeared to be out of place. I chalked it up to my senses being heightened due to my rigorous nighttime training.

As I started to walk back to the computer lab, I noticed a guy in dark sunglasses leaning against a locker outside of the admissions office. He wore a tattered jean jacket, stonewashed jeans, and Doc Martens – a Sid-Vicious-looking wannabe. I went back to my normal workday routine, but I saw this guy everywhere I turned. I thought maybe I was seeing signs where there were only coincidences, but I felt edgy and anxious anyway.

Finally, I snapped, totally out of character for me in my work environment. I turned and cussed the guy out, told him to leave me alone, only not in the kindest of words. I really didn't mean to cause a scene. I could hear the older women in financial aid talking about my colorful language -- heck, one lady was so shocked she didn't even notice her coffee mug overflowing. I didn't want to spook them any further, so I made my way to the cafeteria downstairs. It would be empty at that time of day. The punk followed me, close on my heels. I whirled around quickly to face him, hoping to throw him off. He didn't even flinch.

"Excuse me," I said, locking eyes with him and setting my gaze. Silence -- just an eerie smile. "Yo, can I help you with something?"

He smiled. "It was hard to track you down, but the boss will be pleased with my efforts nonetheless." Boss? Who the heck is this loser? Suddenly his voice changed to that of a hiss.

"I'm sorry, but this is it for you." Everything in me went cold and my hair stood on end. He removed his dark sunglasses and revealed bright glowing purple eyes.

"Cut the crap," I boldly shouted, putting two and two together. "You're one of the Madonna, aren't you?"

The guy began to chuckle, an unpleasant, wheezing sound. "Not quite. I'm no Madonna, but I won't need that kind of power to take you out." He raised his bony fingers and snapped.

With that, the school cafeteria became dark, aged, and covered with dust and cobwebs. The fluorescent lights in the halls dimmed and sporadically flickered. The long wooden tables were now moldy and cracked, with moss snaking through every seam. Rust accumulated on the chrome stools, and the scent of stale food whispered through the air. Above our heads, the stained tile ceiling was cast in the sick yellow tint of a lifetime smoker's fingers. We were alone.

"What the hell is this? Answer me!"

The punk looked at me and began to giggle. "This, Transient, is Antithesis Magic. It takes way too much energy to produce my true form here on Terra. This is a space we Pooka use so we can save our energy and really be ourselves."

With this brief explanation, his body grew immensely buff, and his skin changed from a pinkish hue to a stale gray. His face stretched out like the snout of an alligator, and a set of fangs began to grow, overlapping his top and bottom lips.

"What in the world is a Pooka?" I thought. But never mind that, I wasn't sure if I was ready for a real fight. Sure, training in the Usugurai helped, but who was I kidding? However, this punk wasn't leaving me much time for self-doubt. I had to do something -- anything.

The creature lunged, swiping at me with his long, bear-like claws. Far too close for comfort, but I avoided his assault by jumping out of the way.

"Oh, you've got some speed to ya," he hissed.

He lunged at me in a corkscrew motion. Just as I jumped back, the punk drilled into the ground in front of me like a machine. I barely had time to blink before he burst out of the ground behind me, swiping my back with his claws. I had never experienced pain like that before. I fell to the ground in agony.

"Oh, what's wrong?" he hissed. "Are you having trouble keeping up?"

He dove into the ground again like an Olympic swimmer, tattered linoleum cracking and curling around the gaping hole. Oh, crap not again! This time he came out to my right, and I tried everything I could to dodge. The punk slashed me right in the ribs.

I screamed in pain. That one got me good.

I'm losing blood, no way I can keep this up, I thought with panic. Then I remembered: The toothbrush Preston gave me! Time to put this thing to good use!

"You're pretty tough, I'll give you that," I gasped, furtively reaching for the toothbrush.

The punk gave me a look of disappointment and snarled, "Ah, Maybe Lord Camio is wrong about you. You're all bark, no bite." At that moment I drew my secret weapon, and the punk's loud laugh echoed the ghastly halls. "Wait, a toothbrush? You plan on killing me...with a toothbrush..." the punk collapsed into laughter. "Now that you mention it, I think I have a cavity that needs some attention -- or maybe you can give me a lecture on how to floss."

My face turned beet red. "Shut your stupid mouth! It's called a disguise, and it wasn't my idea!" I focused every piece of energy I had left into the palm of my hand, and bam! Sardna appeared. The punk looked perplexed.

"What manner of trickery is this?"

"This, you stupid lizard, is Sardna," I proudly exclaimed. "Now let's finish this."

The Punk dove back into the ground and burst through the floor in front of me, jumping ten feet into the air. It was impressive, but there was no way I was going to let him catch me a third time. I stepped back on a pivot and blocked his gruesome claws with Sardna. I could feel the power coursing through my body. Then I remembered Preston's training, and his guiding words were echoing in my memory. Próvlepsi! I forced the punk back with my block. He lunged forward and ran across the wall to my left, cracking the subway tile as he sprung off with his claws. "Focus, Tyler," I murmured to myself.

I located it: his weak spot, a small glowing area right above his navel. Just as the creature leapt off the wall, his claws hastening toward me, I drove Sardna square into his weak spot. The punk bellowed out in pain and turned into ashes. I immediately collapsed to the floor. I was definitely banged up. My eyes began to fill with tears of triumph and exhaustion.

"I … did it. I DID IT! I actually did it!"

I couldn't believe my eyes. The room slowly faded from the haunted image of decay back into the college cafeteria. Gone were the moldy lunch tables and foul stench, replaced with the smell of cheesesteaks and hot grease. Students were now gathered around me, turning politely away as I caught their eyes staring. How long was I in that place? I must look foolish sitting on the floor. My clothes were tattered from head to toe. I bet I looked like I got into a fight with a meat slicer and lost.

I thought about what I had just experienced, the fight I had nearly been destroyed in, but narrowly won, thanks to Preston. My training was paying off. But what was I going to do if the Madonna showed up? I was so sore, and on the verge of blacking out. I could have slept for days, right there on that floor. How the heck was I going to go back to work like this? If Natalie saw me, she would probably think I had a drug problem on top of being incompetent.

Ugh, what in the world am I going to do, how am I going to explain this one? I racked my tired brain for ideas. So, Natalie, I was carrying a computer and then...? I looked like a scratching post for a pet tiger.

In that moment, as I had grown to expect, a puff of purple smoke filled the air around me. I felt my world spinning and fell flat on my face. The smoke cleared and I was back in my house-slash-castle, but I didn't smell the familiar scene of mangos that announced Marie's arrival. I laid there on the floor, waiting to accept my fate.

"Wow, you look like dog crap."

Her sister Emily was standing over me, looking simultaneously bored and smug. She finished up a text on her phone and slipped it into her pencil skirt pocket with a perfectly manicured hand. With her large black wings suspended behind her, she looked like a Victoria's Secret runway model from hell.

"It's nice to see you, too, Emily. Where's Marie? What's happening?"

"Relax," Emily replied, "I'm not here to play house. I'm here to heal your wounds."

Emily raised her bird-like wings and shot a ray of light out of a strange tattoo that had now manifested in her palm. My body floated up off the ground. I felt warm energy throughout my limbs, which started glowing. My body, my clothes, the scratches -- everything was restored. I was healed! I never would have guessed Emily had this kind of power.

"Emily, that was, for lack of a better word, amazing. I had no idea you could do that."

Emily rolled her eyes as if I had said something stupid.

"It's just minor healing magic, it's pretty simple. Good thing I was in the area -- my favorite coffee place is just down the street."

"Hold on!" I exclaimed, "How did you know where I was? Is that some sort of demonic psychic power?"

"Don't be silly. As I said, I was in the area, and Marie asked that I check on you. We all know how tough training can be." I guessed that made sense, but I still had questions -- mostly about the creep that ambushed me.

"Hey Emily, what's a Pooka?" I blurted out.

Emily let out a great sighing laugh. "Pooka are annoying lesser creatures that will do anything to obtain a master or money. They're very weak and usually take on petty crime jobs. Usually Pooka don't go after bounties. This one must have been promised something really special."

"Hm, lesser creatures," I mumbled, "Well, what about this Ant-ithe-sis Magic?"

"That's archaic magic; no one uses that stuff anymore except lesser beings, it's so yesterday."

"Right," I replied, "...So yesterday..."

I had to know more, so I continued to press. "So, I take it you and Marie don't use Ant-ithe-sis Magic." Based off of the look on her face, it was another stupid question. She rolled her eyes, reapplying her lipstick.

"God you never stop, do you, Tyler. My siblings and I don't need to use Antithesis Magic. Our Demon levels are high enough to maintain our human forms without some weird alternate realm." She snapped her compact shut.

"Besides, it's way too filthy there, and these are thousand-dollar shoes."

Like all good things, the healing light-bath had come to an end, and Emily sent me back to the office.

Later that night, I took a little time-out from training and creature-slaying to be a dad. I was due for a bit of normalcy. I played video games with Harley and bashed trucks with Logan, while Marie laid on the couch reading her tablet, a snoring Bronx draped across her legs.

I have to admit, it's a bit odd being the father of two little Demons. Sometimes they played video games, sometimes they would swing their tails around and fly. The day before, I had discovered that Logan could blow fire. Then I learned that Harley could teleport just like her mother.

I was finding that simply being around Marie was odd. On the one hand, she was such a mom, doing homework with the kids, going to Toddler Time, the gym, keeping our house/castle in order and more, on top of working full-time. On the other, she was a centuries-old Demon dedicated to searching out and finding this broken sword in order to save her father. I wondered when she had time to sleep, or if she slept at all. It gave me a new appreciation for everything she did around here.

Wow, life is so different now, I thought, watching my kids laughing together. I probably should appreciate these moments while they last. Man, this has been a rough Monday.

I was exhausted and ready to call it a night. And then a knock came on the door.

It was eight o'clock, too late for a casual visitor. I glanced through the foggy peephole. Preston. After weeks of training in Usugurai, I wasn't used seeing him in his human form, which I found wimpy by comparison.

"Come on in, what's up?"

"Well I've got some good news and better news," Preston said.

"Yeah? let's hear it," chimed Marie as Logan pulled her pant leg.

"Well," said Preston, "I found a shard of the sword." I could barely contain my excitement. This was a huge step forward for us. "And, it only gets better! The shard is in Tokyo!"

"Tokyo?! As in, anime, giant robots, Godzilla, gotta catch 'em all, power up, mighty morphin', kawaii kitty, Tokyo?!" My face lit up like a child's. I think I may have actually been bouncing a little bit.

"Yes, Tokyo!" Preston grinned. "I've been able to detect high energy levels in that region."

"Speaking of the shards," I asked, still bursting with glee, "How do you locate them, anyways?"

Preston smiled, and pulled what appeared to be a large diamond out of his vintage leather jacket pocket.

"Wow, what the heck, man, you're like, rich!" I screamed.

Preston covered his face with his hand and took a deep breath. With a tone of infinite patience, he explained, "Tyler, this is a Windfall Stone. It allows us to pinpoint the shard's location, now that they've basically woken up, thanks to you. However, it can't give us an exact location. Only you can do that."

"Well, pack your bags," Marie said, smiling at me. "We're off to Tokyo."

"This is going to be amazing! I've always wanted to go to Tokyo!" I was bouncing again.

"I know, you nerd," Marie said playfully.

"Wait, how are we going to get there? We don't have that kind of money."

This time it was Marie's turn to look at me as if I had said something stupid.

"Wait!" I shouted, trying to connect the dots on my own, "You can teleport us, right?"

"Sorry, sweets," Marie said. "Unfortunately, teleportation for me is limited to a certain amount of distance."

"So, we're pretty much stuck." What a bummer. There go my dreams of seeing Tokyo.

"Not exactly, Tyler," said Preston, "We'll just have to use the Wanderlust lockets."

"What the heck is that?" I asked.

"Oh sweets, the Wanderlust locket is a piece of Angel tech that can send you just about anywhere you want here on Terra," Marie said.

"Wander...lust lockets? That's an interesting term. Well, hold on, Marie, where do I get one?"

Marie smiled seductively and slipped her arm around my waist. "Oh, you don't need one, cakes. You just have to hold on to me, really, really tight." She grabbed my butt and leaned in to nibble on my earlobe. It was a little awkward, with her brother standing right there, but he seemed to take no notice. God, were all Demons so kinky? But there was no time to reflect on that (as much as I wanted to). We were off to Tokyo.

I had the feeling this would be no ordinary family vacation.

IV
Tokyo Flower

Just a week ago, I had never even been out of the state. Now here I was, in Tokyo. It felt like the most beautiful place I would ever see with my own eyes. It was awesome.

I'll tell you what *wasn't* awesome, though: traveling via Wanderlust Lockets. Imagine your body being nuked like a pizza roll for three minutes in a poorly built microwave. I could feel my insides bubbling and slowly rising in my mouth like the crust of my favorite cheese pizza. Up and down, round and round, dizzy doesn't even scratch the surface of what these lockets do. And the landing…oh, the landing. It felt like I was being shot out of one of those T-shirt cannons at a baseball game. I'm pretty sure I'll never get used to it.

According to Preston's Windfall Stone, the shard of Grus that landed in Tokyo was located in Japan's Sakura National Park. I was impressed with how effortless it had seemed for his to uncover the information on this shard. We were outside of a subway entrance, and crowds of people were flowing in and out of it as the three of us discussed our next move.

"So, do we just grab the stone and that's it?" I asked Marie. "I mean, that seems pretty simple." But I wasn't about to question simple. I was dying to grab the shard quickly, so I could go sightseeing in Tokyo's Akihabara district. I mean, who wouldn't want to go there? The buzzing neon signs, the packed arcade centers, its wall-to-wall video game and electronics stores. It was like a smorgasbord of sensory overload with a side of otaku. On second thought, I would probably have to drag Marie there kicking and screaming; she hated video games. In fact, just before we left for Tokyo, she had turned my PlayStation controller into a toad. She thinks she's *so* funny. Joke's on her, though. I have five controllers.

"Oh sweets, you'll have time for your silly games...and five controllers, huh?" Marie's voice echoed in my head.

"Hey! I thought I told you, Marie, stay out of my head!"

"Do some laundry every once in a while, and maybe I will!" shot back Marie, this time out loud.

"Easy, easy, you two," Preston interjected, "We have work to do. The Windfall Stone has put us in the right direction. Unfortunately, only *you* can see the shard, Tyler." Well, that was a bummer. I guessed I had better get to work. I had been hoping I would at least get a little bit of time to explore, but before I could even blink, we were on the hunt for this shard.

"I think it's best that we stick together on this one," Preston suggested. "None of us are familiar with Tokyo, and the last thing we need to do is get separated. We have to be on our guard. Something feels off since we've arrived."

I'd never seen Preston like this in his human form. He was usually more laid-back, less alpha. But today he seemed attentive, alert. It reminded me of the Preston I knew in his Demon form, the one teaching me to keep my defenses up as we sparred on Acheron. I still wasn't one hundred percent clear on this whole shard business, but what I did know was, if I wanted Marie's father to stay alive, I needed to find them.

As we navigated through Japan's famous Tokyo Metro Station, I couldn't shake the feeling that we were being watched, like someone was following us and keeping close tabs. As we boarded the train, I noticed a little boy sitting with his mother. He reminded me of my own little monsters back home. I allowed myself to zone out, day-dreaming about things to come.

"Tyler, Tyler!" Marie gave me a nudge, "This is our stop." As I focused back in on my surroundings, I could feel that uncanny sensation again that someone was watching, but nothing looked out of place.

What in the world is triggering these feelings? Is this something that will come with a better understanding as I train? I have so many questions, but I know that now is not the time. Marie, Preston and I worked our way to the surface amid the crowds of commuters and made our way to Sakura National Park. As we entered the Garden, I saw a boy standing by the entrance crying. Marie had noticed him, too, and made her way over to him.

She gently approached the child and used her magic to translate back and forth from Japanese to English. "Are you okay?"

"I'm lost!" the boy wept, "And I can't find my mom!"

"How about you and Preston head for the shard, I'll get him to the authorities to find his mother." I smiled to myself. Marie had always had a soft spot for children.

Preston and I slowly made our way through the Park. The trees were in full bloom, the pinkish white petals dancing at the tip of each branch. The grass was trimmed with barber-like precision. Families gathered on blankets enjoying the warm weather, while teens snapped selfies as they crossed the egg-white bridge arcing over the pond. It was gorgeous, but I knew I had work to do. I tried to focus on seeing the shard, whatever it looked like. "What exactly am I looking for?" I began to ask Preston, but my words trailed off. My skin began to feel warm. Soon, I was breaking into a sweat. It felt as if my body were a million degrees.

"You seem sick," Preston exclaimed, "We must be close to the shard!" Well, this was going to suck; I didn't plan on getting the damn flu every time we got close to a shard. As we walked through the park, in front of us loomed a giant tree. It was drastically different from the rest of the trees in the garden; its branches were massive, stretching out as if it were yawning. The roots of the tree rippled and waved through the soil, and there was no grass within the massive trunk's circumference. It felt almost fairytale-like in its presence. It also had a unique smell, a sweet intoxicating aroma that seduced my senses. Oddly enough, for its strange size and nature, no one in the park seemed to acknowledge it. Maybe that's why it called to me, seeking the attention it lacked.

"P, do you hear that?"

"Hear what?"

"Singing. It's beautiful," I breathed. It reminded me of the way my mother used to sing as she cooked in the kitchen when I was a kid, but it was more of a falsetto. Was I the only one that could hear it? In that moment, I understood what I was feeling in my bones. "Preston. The shard is in the tree." As I approached it and placed my hand on its trunk, I could feel the warmth of the shard pulsating under my palm.

As if it was responding to my call, the shard slowly worked its way out of the trunk, through the layers of bark, and into my hand. It was beautiful: sleek and silver in color, polished to a mirror finish. I could see my reflection. *Now that's one handsome nerd,* I joked to myself. All this time I thought it would look like a normal shard of steel. "Preston, this is amazing, are you seeing this? Preston?" I looked up and my heart pounded with fear. Preston had started to nod off, falling flat on his face in the middle of the park. He looked as though he hadn't slept in days. "I... I... feel kin...da...slee..py," he yawned.

"Hold on, P. " I shouted. "You gotta stay up!"

"No—r-run..." his last words were cut into by another giant yawn.

"What?"

"Run... Ma...don...na."

Madonna, here? Where, who? In a panic I whirled to look around me. The park entrance was suddenly overgrown with flowers and vines and a pinkish mist was hanging in the air. The park transformed around me, becoming dark and overgrown, green as far as the eye could see, with no visible markers of the paths that were around us moments ago. How in the world was I going to get out of there?

A mysterious figure appeared from behind a cluster of trees. "Who are you?" I shouted.

A woman's fair voice replied, "Oh, I'm sure you know exactly who I am. Don't play coy." The figure came out of the shadows. It was a woman with short red hair in which was woven a sort of tiara made of fresh flowers, their papery petals fluttering in the wind. She wore a green military-style trench coat unbuttoned over a crop top, which would have made her look tough and rigid, were it not for the sharp contrast of the delicate flowers. She walked toward me, and I could hear the click-clack of her cowboy boots against the hard soil. The air was still and quiet around us. Even though moments ago I had been engulfed in heat and sweating bullets, my skin grew cold and clammy as she approached.

"I am called Flower, Flower of the Madonna. Hand over that shard, and I'll make your death quick. I'll even provide the wreath for your casket." She chuckled. It was an eerie, mirthless laugh.

My stomach began to turn. I knew I was in big trouble, but I had no idea what to do. Inwardly I shrugged and decided to do what I did best: fake it 'til I make it. Putting my shoulders back and widening my stance, I psyched myself into looking fearless.

"Look, lady, I didn't come all the way to Tokyo just so you and your wacko boss can take the shard and kill me," I replied.

"First and foremost, you address me as Sir! I am no lady!" the Flower shouted.

Slowly I reached for my toothbrush, snugly tucked away in the back pocket of my ash-colored skinny jeans. The Flower burst into laughter. "Why on Earth do you have a toothbrush? I mean, what is that going to do?! My smile is already elegant enough, wouldn't you say?"

"IT WASN'T MY IDEA!" I screamed. *I really need Preston to change this; a locket, a watch, anything but a toothbrush.* "Listen, sir, I'll respect your wish, but I can't let you have this shard. If you want it, you'll have to fight me for it!" I couldn't believe how brave I sounded, but what choice did I have? I quickly revealed the toothbrush as Sardna and gripped the hilt tightly, raising the sword in front of me.

"Aren't you full of surprises. Well, since you're making this difficult for me," the Flower responded, "I'll take my time killing you."

I looked over at Preston lying helpless in a field of roses. "Don't worry about your friend, I'm sure he'll bounce back. It is only one sleeping dart. Right now, Merozantine, you're all mine. I'm a one-man guy – call me old-fashioned," the Flower said with a grin.

I knew this fight would be a loss, but my pride believed otherwise. I grabbed my blade and lunged toward the Flower, swinging with every fiber in my being, and I still missed. He was so fast, it seemed as if he simply sidestepped. At one point he even caught my blade and held it frozen in place between the tip of his index finger and thumb, balancing me in mid-air as if I were a piece of paper. I felt something slithering up my spine, but before I could determine whether it was a snake or my sweat or God knows what, I was paralyzed. It was a vine, wrapping around my neck and lifting my feet off the ground. I could feel my arms going limp as I dropped Sardna and the shard onto the grass.

"My, my, aren't we are in trouble," mocked the Flower. "What to do with you now? I have an idea! Let's see how tough your ribs are! But first I'll take this shard." He picked up the shard and placed it gently inside his crop top.

This is a little kinky, but if only I could get my hand in there, maybe I could swipe it back.

I was sure then that I was done for. I looked over at Preston, for all intents and purposes dead to the world. He was fogging up the grass with his mouth wide open, drooling in his sleep.

The Flower began to punch me in the stomach in tandem with his speech. "Oh... (WACK)...this...(PAP)...is...(POW)... so... (WACK)...much...(POW)...fun!" Every punch to my stomach felt as if my insides were going to spill out of my back. The Flower then slammed me to the ground and begin to stomp me in a similarly rhythmic fashion. I felt myself fading out of consciousness as my insides popped and squished in sickening succession. "I think I heard some bones crack! How funny, it sounds like sticks over an open flame!" This guy was clearly a sadist. My vision began to go black, but I fought to stay awake. The Flower lifted me from the ground and punched me in the face repeatedly. My eyes began to swell shut. "Look at this, I can't believe how squishy humans are," laughed the Flower. I'd never experienced pain such as this. Preston wasn't lying when he said these guys were strong.

"Marie..." I tried to speak, but this beating he was handing out wasn't helping.

"What's that?" said the Flower, "Oh, I see you're hoping your sexy wife will come to your rescue. I can assure you she has her hands full." Flower then raised his right hand and gathered a bundle of vines in the air. The vines formed into a humanoid shape, gradually weaving and forming into a little boy, except this one was made entirely of leaves and vines. I wondered briefly if that was what the crying boy really looked like, if he ever really had human skin and clothes at all, or if the pile of sticks and leaves was enchanted to make us see what Flower had wanted us to see.

"I'm sure as we speak, he's turning into one of my Rhizomes. And silly me, I forgot to feed him," he laughed. "Hey, I have a nasty good idea," exclaimed the Flower. "Why don't we get front row seats, I mean you shouldn't miss the show! Tell you what, let's take a look through the eyes of my Rhizomes. Doesn't that sound just fabulous?" The Flower said with delight. Then he raised his free hand and launched what seemed to be a giant seed into the air. The seed burst into a wall of white light.

The Flower turned my attention to the glowing white wall. It had the quality of a grainy old horror movie: buildings, people, and then -- Marie! My aching and beaten body filled with fear. She had fallen for his trap without a second thought. If only she could hear my thoughts. The screen crackled and shuddered every few seconds, like it was struggling to keep a connection. *God, would it have killed this guy to at least give me 4K? I mean if you're gonna make me watch, at least make it clear.*

"I want you to watch this," snarled the Flower, "It's going to be a masterpiece!"

All I could do now was watch and pray as Marie bent down and took the boy's hand.

"So little guy, where are you from," Marie asked. "I bet you really miss your mommy, huh?"

"I do," whimpered the boy.

"You know back home, I have a little one about your age," said Marie. "Don't you worry, we're going to find your mom. Actually, come to think of it, what is your name?"

The boy's face took a mischievous turn. His voice became raspy, his teeth turned into sharp files. "My name? I've never had lunch ask for my name," growled the boy. His shirt ripped apart, his pants tore from seam to seam. He grew into a hulking beast, with the face of that of a Venus flytrap, the veins in his muscles pulsing with a purple ooze.

People in the area began to panic and scream, shoving each other out of the way to run far from the monster.

"My father gave me specific instructions," snarled the plant-like creature.

Marie smiled with confidence, "And what exactly would that be, my green gruesome friend?"

He roared thunderously, "To eat you alive, and not to leave a single bone!" The Rhizome lunged at Marie and grabbed her. He slammed her into the side of a building, then tossed her into the air. As Marie's body flew into the sky, the creature vanished into thin air and reappeared above her, kicking her body back onto the street. Marie's body bounced off the pavement like a rubber ball, with a thunderous smack.

"Oh my, that looks painful," he snarled. "But I do so like to tenderize my meat, it makes for easy digestion." He grabbed Marie and began to squeeze. She gazed back at him with no expression. "What's the matter, bitch, weak with fear?" he asked.

Marie cracked a smile. Then she began to laugh hysterically.

"Shut up!" he screeched, "It's time to die!"

With his free hand, the beast wrapped his gruesome claws around Marie's neck. The few bystanders that had remained watched in horror, but the claws around her neck were swallowed by a cloud of dust. As it slowly cleared, anticipation drew within the crowd of onlookers. But Marie was gone. "What! Where did she go?!" he shouted.

"God, you really are a bore," said Marie from upon the Rhizome's shoulder. Through my pain, I laughed at the image of Marie on the screen. She had the same authoritative look and pose when she was corralling our kids at home. She was such a mom, even now.

"Get off of me!" shouted the Rhizome, as he swiped for Marie. She quickly dodged. "Hold still," he whined, as he hammered his fist toward her. In a flash, Marie had her hands around the creature's fist. He tugged and tugged. "Let me go!" he screamed petulantly. "What the heck, lady, why are you so strong?"

"Oh, you poor baby," taunted Marie, "And here I thought I was a bitch? Oh hey, by the way, do you need this?"

"Need what?" asked the monster.

Marie responded matter-of-factly: "This arm," as she proceeded to rip the arm of the monster clean from his prodigious body. Purple ooze splashed Marie's face and chest.

"Ahhh! Just wait till that grows back," cried the creature as he dropped to he knees in agony.

"Aww," said Marie, glancing down at herself, "This stain will never come out. This was a brand-new cardigan! Though I suppose I could try to bleach it…" The monster was wailing with pain, clutching the place where his arm used to be. Marie acted as though she didn't hear him – again I thought of her with the kids, tacitly ignoring their attention-seeking tantrums as she folded the laundry.

"So, monster, what's your Father's play?" she asked, brushing the dirt from her nails off on her tattered cardigan. "If you wish to keep your life, I think you'd better start talking."

"Oh, haha," the creature grumbled. "It's far too late, by now your little Transient boy-toy, and your pathetic excuse for a demon brother, are probably dead at father's feet. We knew sleep darts wouldn't work on you; we're well aware of your knowledge of magical antidotes and quick repellents. So, we had to flush you out."

Marie's face broke into a grin. "Well, I guess we're done here then."

The monster's eyes grew wide with fear, "Wait no, I… I can help! Trust me."

Marie began to chant something I could only partially understand. "Uhtceare Jaws of erstwhile ways, bring forth the eald dark flames." At this, the pavement began to shake and crack. A great roaring black flame engulfed the monster, its screams echoing down the city street and reverberating between the buildings.

"I have to get back to Tyler and Preston. If that monster was telling the truth…Hold on, sweets, I'm coming!"

The white screen hovering in the sky above us burst into a ball of white flames. Marie's energy must have been so powerful it caused the screen to self-destruct. The embers from the burst rained down upon the Flower and I, setting ablaze a patch of roses by our feet. The Flower's darkened with anger. "Look at what your stupid little girlfriend has done! My poor Rhizome, he...he was just a seedling! Well now, I guess that leaves me with only one choice."

Oh god, why did I get the feeling that this one choice wasn't a hug. The Flower tossed my limp body against a tree. I landed on the grass and managed to roll over, only to see a shadow looming in the air above my body. BAM! The Flower landed flat on my stomach, jamming his knee into my gut.

As I lay pinned underneath him, he leaned into my ear. "You're beginning to bore me, old sport," he said, as he quickly rose to his feet and kicked me across the garden.

I felt so useless, being far too injured to help myself, let alone Preston.

Preston, please wake up, do something! My thoughts were racing, but I was too battered to speak. The Flower grabbed me by my neck and lifted me off the ground. "Take a good look, Transient, because I can assure you it's your last." I struggled to see through my swollen eyelids. I believed it was the end and felt tears stinging my eyes. I would never see my beautiful kids again. As I drifted out of consciousness, a puff of purple smoke appeared.

I know that smell. That's a mango, and where there is a mango, there's Marie. "Okay, Madonna," Marie shouted from across the garden. "You've had your fun, now drop my sweets!" *Such a stupid nickname, so very, very stupid,* I thought, able to cringe even with blood pooling my insides, but I'd never been happier to hear it.

The Flower dropped me like a hot pan and seemed to almost rejoice.

"Camio and Loath and their stupid shard can wait. Now it's a party!" shouted the Flower.

"Be careful what you wish for, lady," Marie shouted.

"You silly bitch!" screamed the Flower, "I'm not a lady, but I'll be more than happy to beat the ignorance out of your face." I had to be honest, I knew this lady preferred to be addressed as a man, but I'd never been beaten up by a better-smelling person. It was like a bottle of cucumber avocado shampoo beat the crap out of me. But I was going off the rails again. Must have been all the brain damage I sustained. My body hurt like hell. Hopefully Marie could finish this guy off. To say that Preston and I were in bad shape was the understatement of the century.

"So, answer me this, Madonna," said Marie, cracking her knuckles. "Are Camio and Loath enjoying their little stint of power on Empyrean?"

The Flower laughed derisively. "What does it matter? Soon you, your filthy siblings, your stupid husband, and your loser of a father will be dead."

Marie glared at the Flower, "How do you sleep at night, knowing that you were once under my father's command, and now you serve a genocidal maniac? It seems that the apples that fall farthest from the tree taste the shittiest."

The Flower dashed across the wide green field, grabbed Marie by the throat and slammed her into the ground. *This doesn't look good*, I thought. The Flower lifted Marie off the ground by her neck, but Marie's expression was blank. "Why don't we stop the nonsense and cut to the chase."

"I thought you'd never ask," croaked Marie. She easily broke free from Flower's clutch and jumped back a few feet. The two seemed to stare into each other's very soul with hatred.

The ground began to shake, and roots emerged from the hard soil, encasing the Flower in what appeared to be a pod. The pod glowed a hot red, and as the petals unfolded, a new monster emerged. It was Flower, but he no longer looked like a pretty redhead in a flower tiara and trench coat. A metallic breast plate covered his chest, leaving his torso exposed. His legs were now covered by bright green chain mail, and the tiara on his head was now a helmet with a rose in its center. The Flower reached out his hand and a long gold trident appeared. I had to admit, this fashion upgrade was impressive.

Marie's voice magically popped in my head, *"Sweets, Sweets, can you hear me?"*

"I can, but barely. I'm just too sore to focus."

"Here's the plan, my sexy man. I'm going to transfer you a tad of my energy. I need you to grab Preston, and you two get out of here."

Everything felt hazy. *"But what about you?"* I pleaded.

Marie snapped her fingers, and a surge went through my body.

"I'll be fine," Marie responded in my mind, her voice gentle and a little bit sad. *"Look, Sweets, the truth is, I can't win this fight. Even if I go to my max, I'm not strong enough to stay in this form to fight him."*

"Wait, so all of this is…"

"Yes, a bluff, now get out of here."

"Marie I can't!"

"SWEETS, GO!"

With my new surge of energy, I limped over to Preston's snoozing body. *I gotta get us out of here,* I thought, *I have a feeling this is going to get nasty.* I pulled him up by his T-shirt, throwing his gangly arm over my battered shoulder. "Well, Sleepytime, we gotta dip. I hope your sister knows what she's doing."

Marie's eyes began to glow a bright gold, she was morphing into her Demon form. However, something was different this time. Gone was the long black hair, traded in for a fiery red mane. Her golden horns were also gone, and her body was now covered in an intricate pattern of runes. Her six-inch black heels were now metal gladiator style sandals and her medallion was glowing, now fused into her chest. Her wings, which had been bird-like, now looked more like that of a bat's, with large claws protruding out of them. She wore large silver gauntlets on her arms with sharp metal wings attached to them. But her eyes: when I saw them, I felt my chest get tighter. Her eyes were human and yet something was different; it was like the life and love had been drained from them. These were the eyes of pure evil. Marie dashed through the cherry blossom trees, punching The Flower square in his face, a trail of scorched earth in her wake. The Flower's body whistled as it flew into the side of a fountain now overgrown with brush. The Flower got to his feet, brushing the rubble off of his once pristine chain mail. "Finally, a challenge! Your boy toy didn't put up much of a fight! But this; this is special!"

Flower drew his trident and launched it like a javelin at Marie. Marie deflected the trident in a single swipe, but as she did, Flower appeared beside her, kicking her square in the jaw. The magnitude of the kick caused waves that knocked Preston and me off of our feet.

This kind of power is insane, if these two keep this up they're going to destroy the entire park, I thought. Marie rose to her feet and the two began to fight furiously in an airborne barrage, trading punch for punch, kick for kick. "Hey, P. I don't know if you can hear me, brother, but I think we may stand a chance! Marie is holding her own." Or at least that was what I thought.

The two crash-landed on the grass, an eerie silence coming over the charred and broken battleground.

"Well, you are a lot stronger than before, I'll give you that. But how long do you think you can sustain that power?" Flower grinned, slowly rising up off the ground.

Marie stood up as well, brushing an errant strand of hair from her face. I'd never seen her like this before, no humor, no witty come-back, just blank. It was as if her soul was completely gone -- if demons even had souls. I realized then that I wasn't sure.

Marie lunged towards The Flower, but something was different now. She seemed to be slowing down; the Flower was gaining the upper hand. Something was going terribly wrong and I could feel it. Marie was breathing heavily.

"What's wrong, beautiful? Running out of steam? Nice try, but you know we higher-ranking Demons can use our Max Power far longer than you second-class losers. You're just trying to buy time, by using yours. Very risky," admonished the Flower. "But just know, it won't save your sexy little human toy. Once I'm finished with you, I'm going to savor breaking him!"

"Wait, what Max Power? It is possible that Marie and her family can become more powerful than they already are?" I murmured to myself. I heard a familiar grumble. It was Preston. He was finally conscious.

"Ugh, I believe I can answer that," he groaned.

"Preston! You're okay!"

"I'll make this quick, because we don't have much time," he said, shaking off his deep sleep with a vigorous nod. "Some Angels and Demons can push their power to a point that it moves the mark, even if only temporarily. Only immensely strong Empyreans can maintain their Maximum Power on Terra for extended periods of time. The Madonna are B-class demons, so this is an easy task for them. Marie and I are C-class."

What! C? Is he joking?

"Now, Marie has maxed out her power."

"Okay," I said urgently, "So just how strong is Marie now?"

"Well, at Max Power she is about a B-class Demon, but…"

"But what, Preston, come on, man!" I was terrified to find out what this meant for my Marie. I had a feeling she was in serious danger.

Preston's tone became somber. "She can't maintain this form for long. And as you can see, she's not herself. Only with proper training can one have control while using Max Power."

I could feel a new level of hopelessness weighing on my weary shoulders. "Preston, be honest with me. Remember the creature that attacked me at work?"

"Yes," Preston said.

"What was its level?"

Preston turned into his large Demon form and dropped to one knee. "Tyler, you can't think like that."

"No, Preston, tell me," I murmured.

Preston sighed, "Pooka are usually considered Nether beings, so weak they don't qualify for even F-class."

"What? Ouch. Well, that makes me feel just stellar."

"But you can't focus on that Tyler, you must give it time, you'll grow stronger, faster and become a better fighter with practice and patience."

Time was just what we didn't have right now. Marie was growing weaker. She dashed toward the Flower, but he was way too fast. The Flower flipped through the air and landed behind Marie, using the blunt end of his trident to whack Marie across the field. "What a hit!" the Flower laughed. Marie's body went flying, bouncing off the ground like a stone across a pond. She managed to stumble to her feet, only to be met by the Flower's fist. The Flower grabbed Marie by her throat, slamming her body into the ground like an old teddy bear.

We watched helplessly from a distance. Marie was giving it her all, but her power was beginning to subside. Her long black hair, two golden horns, and regal epaulets were returning. I couldn't believe my eyes. She looked so helpless, and here I was, sidelined. What kind of man was I? I was never big on gender roles, heck, sometimes Marie even cut the grass, but no man should ever have to watch his lady be beaten. But what was I going to do? I was a failure. My wife, the mother of my children, was once again putting her neck on the line for me.

I know I'm no Demon or Angel. But there has to be a way to get stronger faster, I can't let this happen ever again! Presuming we get out of this alive. No, screw that noise, we are getting out of this alive!

"You seem to be losing power," snickered the Flower. He began to walk slowly towards Marie. Marie began to chant, "Uhtceare Jaws of erstwhile ways, bring forth the eald dark—"

The Flower grabbed Marie by the throat, cutting her off mid-chant: "Trust, your low-ranking magic will have no effect on me! I will squeeze the life from your disgusting body. Then I'm going to track down every last one of your siblings and turn them into nothing more than smeared bloodstains on this filthy realm!"

"Preston, Marie needs our help, I'm not going to let her die here!" I pulled off what was left of my tattered hoodie and summoned Sardna. "This ends here and now!" Here I was, showing my foolhardy bravery again; still unable to learn my lesson. *Whatever, who cares,* I thought. *This is my wife and I'm not letting her die at the hands of this sadist.*

I ran toward the fight as fast as my body would allow. "Hey!" I shouted.

Flower turned to me gleefully.

"Let my wife go," I firmly said.

"My, my, someone is ready to die. Sadly, you'll have to wait your turn, I'm very busy and important," uttered the Flower.

"Guess you're not man enough for a real fight," I quivered, under my breath.

"What did you say?" The Flower kicked Marie across the field and turned to me in a fit of rage. "I told you about your remarks before, stupid boy. Now you really will die." He lunged toward me. I knew he was too fast to dodge, so I did the only thing I could think to do, I wrapped my arms around him and attempted a tackle. The Flower raised his fist and punched me square in the face. My vision went black.

Lying face down in the dirt, drifting out of consciousness, I heard footsteps coming toward me, then stopping. It was Flower. He was silent a moment, then he said, "As you wish. I have the shard, my Lord." I couldn't understand why he was saying that, and then realized he wasn't speaking to me. The Flower stood over my prone body, nudged me almost affectionately in the ribs with the toe of his boot, and said, "I guess we'll have to play another time." A great hole of light appeared in the middle of the field, and with one good eye I watched the Flower walk into the light and vanish. It was the last thing I saw before being engulfed in total darkness.

I guess this is what death feels like. If not, it must be pretty damn close.

Somewhere far away, a voice was calling me, gentle and familiar.

"Tyler, sweets. Sweets, wake up." I opened my eyes, felt an impulse to sit up quickly, but found I couldn't. My body felt like a ton of bricks was piled onto it. Marie was sitting in front of me with Preston.

"Tyler, how do you feel?" Preston asked.

"Like someone beat me half to death."

Marie's face was overwhelmed with sorrow. I knew that look – it wasn't often that I saw it, but it was the look she got whenever she was about to break down into tears.

"Marie, it's okay," I tried my best to soothe her. I knew, too, that her pride was hurt. Like a cloud darkening the sky, her sorrow quickly turned into rage.

"What are we going to do, Tyler?! How are we supposed to overcome this? We've literally lost everything. This fight, the shard! Everything!" I put my head down gently into Marie's warm lap as she held me. I began to chuckle, weakly, and that soon turned into hysterical laughter. Marie's anger refocused onto me. "What in the world is so funny, Tyler? We almost died, and this was all a total loss." I popped my head up with a Cheshire-cat smile, reached into my pocket and removed a shard.

"Wait, what, how!" shouted Preston and Marie in nearly perfect unison. I began to explain, "Well, remember when the Flower knocked my lights out..." I began laughing again. "I reached into his armor and managed to snag it. Guess the beating was worth it." Marie threw her arms around me, and Preston laughed in relief. "I'm no psychic," I said, gently squeezing Marie around her waist with my one good arm, "But I think it's best if we hit the road. I'm sure the Flower has to be enraged right about now."

One shard down, three to go.

V
D-Town

A month had passed since our little skirmish, if I can call it that, in Tokyo. Life felt almost normal for a change, and all of us seemed comforted by the vague peace that had fallen over our suburban-home-turned-castle. There hadn't been any signals from the remaining shards, and with that trail cold, the mission was at a standstill. Marie's dear old dad, Dave, or I guess I mean Daevas, was still in the hospital. Not much had changed with his mysterious condition, but at least he was stable.

It was a mild Saturday morning in May. Marie was balancing our finances in her tattered journal, Logan was throwing a temper tantrum over something I couldn't even understand through his tears, and Harley was ignoring every word I said, her face buried in a video game. Ahh, the sweet life. Even Demons needed a break from being, well, you know… Demons.

"Hey, Marie?"

Nothing. She was staring at her phone screen.

"Marie!"

I should have known – I was blocked out, playing second fiddle to a nursing video on her Instagram.

"Marie!" I shouted. Her eyes flicked up to meet mine. Finally, some attention. "Hey, why don't we go out tonight? Let's meet up with your family and get drinks or something."

I figured it would cheer her up after everything that had been going on – there was otherwise no way I would subject myself to a night surrounded by all of her siblings at once. It's a little much, especially with alcohol in the mix.

"Oh, that sounds like fun!" Marie replied, her eyes lighting up.

Take my advice: never, ever, *ever* drink with Demons. It's loud, they won't stay in human form, and it's not long before the entire night devolves into chaos. Or maybe this was just how Marie's family was. In-laws, am I right?

In any case, my parents agreed to watch the little monsters, and I headed out to spend time with my Demon wife and her siblings. *Maybe it'll be all right this time, just a normal night out,* I naively thought.

Marie and I were late to the bar as usual. As soon as we walked in, Def Leppard assaulted our ears, blaring out of the jukebox. It was smoky and reeked of Marlboro Reds. There wasn't much life in the joint, just a few scruffy-looking fellows laughing it up and shooting pool in the back. The bartender looked like he could keel over at any moment, shaking cocktails like a chattering skeleton. The red patent leather stools were tattered, revealing cigarette-burned yellow foam cushions. A buzzing neon sign that read "D-Town Inn" hung above the bar. As I looked at it, the D periodically flickered. I remember Marie telling me that this was her father's favorite spot, and he helped open it years ago.

Nicole, Marie's second-oldest sister, greeted us. Naturally, she was already drunk.

"Heyyy! Tyler, what are you drinking?" Nicole slurred, then disappeared into a boozy cloud of purple smoke. It cleared, and she was a Demon floating right in front of my face -- although she seemed to be having a hard time staying upright, overcorrecting from time to

time. I found myself tilting from side to side to maintain eye contact.
"Did I ever tell you this story?" Nicole slurred, splashing her whiskey in my face as she spoke. "You know, when we were little, and
Marie first got her wings..." she suddenly dissolved into a fit of
raucous laughter.

What the hell? That wasn't even a complete story, I thought.

"McKenzie!" Nicole shouted, catching sight of their youngest sister arriving, and stepped awkwardly out of her floating to stride past
us. "MCKENZIE!"

"Oh brother, what a night this is going to be," I muttered under my
breath. A loud screech of laughter rang out across the room. It was
Emily, who was also – you guessed it – drunk as a skunk.

"Hey sis-TER! Ty! How's it going! WANT A DRINK!" Her questions came out like declarative sentences, which in fairness, was
Emily's personality even when she was sober.

"Hey girl!" I replied, in an oddly feminine pitch, warmly receiving
her hug. I might as well have been holding a pumpkin spice latte and
wearing a trendy scarf. Emily had that kind of power: no matter what
you thought about her or what you were feeling like before you saw
her, when she spoke to you, you would match her personality and
energy level despite yourself. I wondered if that had anything to do
with her being a Demon.

"So dearest brother-in-law, first off, I *love* the vintage blazer, and
second, I heard you got your hands on a SHARD!"

"This is true," I replied, "And I see you've invested in more glitter
since the last time we hung out." I was covered after her embrace; I
looked like I had been at a Kesha concert.

"Oh, brother in-law, you're hilarious," she doubled over in a fit of
laughter and tilted her coupe glass as she did, soaking me in something pink. Then, poof! She too, disappeared into a puff of smoke

and reappeared in her true form.

Ugh, why do they insist on being Demons as they drink? I nervously looked around to see if anyone we didn't know had entered the pool room. I didn't exactly feel comfortable with all of these Demons floating around out in the open. And it didn't take long for Marie to ditch me for Captain and Coke.

I wonder what a human would even think if they walked in right about now, I thought. *I mean seriously, this isn't normal, right? Come to think of it, why haven't the guys in the back by the pool table freaked out? Then again, they're so wasted they probably just think Halloween came early. And the bartender, well, he's so old and senile he probably can't tell the difference either. No wonder Marie and her siblings let loose in this hole in the wall.*

God, my mind was moving a million miles per second. I needed to relax.

Now that I'd had whisky and some sort of girly Cosmopolitan spilled on me, I figured I'd try to get a drink inside of me for a change. I made my way to the end of the bar where McKenzie was sitting. "Hey Mac, what's up?" I was dying for small talk.

"Hi, Tyler," she replied gloomily. I wondered if something had happened.

"So, what's new?" As you can see, I'm the master of small talk.

"They always pick the worst bars, but that's not news," she responded drily.

She may be in a foul mood, but at least she's not in her Demon form, I thought.

"Sweets!" came a lusty voice behind me. *Oh god, no.* I looked over my shoulder, and it appeared that Marie had wasted little time throwing back the rum and cokes. If you thought Marie was handsy as a Demon, add a little liquor into the mix, and I pretty much need a restraining order. "So, sweets, you know we can go back to the car," Marie said, draping her arms around me. She was in her demon form already, unsurprisingly. She rubbed a leather-clad leg against my thigh. "Neither one of us has to drive – well, maybe *you* do."

"Um, Marie, didn't we come here to hang out?" I asked.

"Oh, I can make it *hang out*," Marie replied as she licked her lips. And just like that, Marie was using her Demon powers to keep me from getting up from my stool. She knew I hated that; being under Demonic control is literally the worst, especially when Marie drinks. One time she made me cook her tacos at one in the morning while naked. Definitely not my most elegant moment.

Despite all of the drunken Demon shenanigans, the night had been going pretty well. I began to relax and lean into the festivities. Preston even showed up, eventually; I was wondering where he had been all night.

"Hey, hey what's up P.!" Boy, was I was glad he showed up. I needed some male interaction.

"I see my sisters are out of control, per usual," chuckled Preston.

"You're telling me," I said, but Preston, like his sisters, wasn't usually one to shy away from drinking. I couldn't help but wonder what he had been up to that had made him so late to the party.

Preston slowly inched toward me, giving me a nudge with his massive elbow. "Hey, Ty's, can you keep a secret?" he whispered. I nodded my tipsy head in approval. Preston began to slowly scroll through his phone. He pulled up a picture of a beautiful girl. She was worlds shorter than Preston with coffee-colored eyes and chestnut hair.

"Well… What do you think?" Preston asked.

I couldn't believe it, Preston had been on a… date? I tried to gather my thoughts as the liquor was starting to gain control. "Good for you, P. She's cute. I didn't think you would be into...Terra girls."

Preston smiled upon my approval. "Just hope my sisters don't spook her away. They can be a bit rough, ya know." He then proceeded to order the next round, which was met with an eruption of cheers.

When this family drank, it was as if they didn't even give themselves time to *taste* the liquor. But I had to say I was having fun. I actually felt like I was one of them for a change. Unfortunately, the good times wouldn't last long, because suddenly McKenzie stood up from her bar stool where she had been sulking and reverted to her Demon form.

"Guys. Something's wrong," said McKenzie.

As Marie had explained to me once, McKenzie's powers weren't as strong as her siblings', but she did possess this weird ability to sense Angels and Demons from a great distance, particularly if it was someone outside of the family, or someone with bad intentions.

"What do you mean?" Preston replied after a swig of his third beer.

"Just what it sounds like," she snapped. "Something's outside the bar."

Whatever it was, there is always safety in numbers, so we all ran outside to the empty sidewalk. I couldn't help but think the worst: a Madonna. Marie had helped me heal physically from the beating I received in Tokyo, but the memory of it was still sharp in my mind. However, it didn't appear that anything was there, just a really large hawk sitting on a telephone pole. Odd, sure, but no Angel or Demon.

"Some powers you got there," Nicole scoffed.

"Wow, way to make me feel like crap," McKenzie replied tearfully. "I swear something was out here!"

Maybe it was the shard, I thought. Marie and I figured it would be best to keep it close at all times, so we had Nicole cook up a nice little spell to hide the shard in an invisible bubble. It was actually pretty cool.

But now I couldn't divert my attention away from this odd hawk. It slowly turned its brown head, throwing its sharp yellow beak into relief against the night sky.

A bright eye fixed upon us. "Finally, I've found you."

"Okay, what the heck is going on here – demons are one thing, I don't think I can handle talking wildlife, too!" I said. I suddenly felt a strong urge to get another drink.

"So, you are the Merozantine," squawked the hawk.

"Um, are you talking to me?" I replied.

The Hawk cocked his head and looked disapprovingly at Marie. I didn't even know hawks could look disappointed. "Marie, are you sure this boy is the heir to the Merozantine? He seems kind of ..." he trailed off and looked back at me with that same skeptical look. I hadn't known that hawks could look skeptical, either.

Marie's eyes turned hot-tamale-red: "You listen to me, you stupid chicken, don't ever question my sweets!"

"Same old Marie, I see, always opening her fat mouth!" squawked the hawk.

"That's enough, you two," Nicole chimed in. "So, Keith, we're glad you're okay and all, but what's with the costume change, and why are you on Terra?"

"Okay, hang on a second. Do you guys KNOW this...bird?" I asked, incredulous. On second thought, maybe I *had* had enough to drink.

Turns out that Keith had worked for Marie and her siblings as a hired operative. He was once an Angel, one who also mistrusted Camio and Loath's intentions. Once he learned that Marie and her siblings fled the Kingdom in search of the shards, Keith had made it his business to follow them to Oldenburg.

"So, Keith, give us the low-down one more time," gulped Nicole as she chugged her lager.

"Yeah, why are you--" Emily interrupted herself with a loud hiccup, but continued as though nothing had happened, "Ya know, some kinda bird now?"

Keith slowly tilted his head in embarrassment, covering his eyes with a wing.

"Okay, I'll try to explain it slowly this time so you can understand in your, umm, current state," he squawked.

"Heeeyyy," Marie chimed in, "Are you calling us...stupid!"

Keith let out a great sigh. "Just let me tell the story, please!" he shouted. "You see, I discovered a bit of information while you and the others were absent that would prove useful."

It was so hard to focus, and I had the feeling this was going to be a long, drawn-out story. Plus, being drunk was going to test my abilities to converse, so I sat quietly and let the bird tell his tale.

"Each Madonna has a unique weakness," squawked Keith. "A weakness that, when exploited, could turn the tide in a fight. I was coming here to find you and give you this valuable information. But upon reaching Terra, I was ambushed by two Madonna. One of them was the Wolf. They somehow were aware of my arrival. While locked in combat with the Wolf, I was tricked into destroying innocent creatures. Creatures that had nothing to do with our war, and I had burned them to a crisp. Thanks to the Wolf, my rage had gotten the best of me. She's as cunning as she is deadly. So, in return, this is my penance."

I could feel that this was a sore spot for Keith; I couldn't imagine dealing with that kind of guilt.

"I will remain in this form, until I discover a way to restore that forest and all of its creatures."

We now had the whole scoop: not one but two Madonna here on Terra, an Angel paying for his sins by taking the form of a hawk. Everything seemed to go from odd to just ridiculous. But I should have been used to that by now, right? Only now it didn't fill me with a sort of detached irony; it was making me mad. Nothing seemed to be improving for us – this Angel might have taken on and beaten the Madonna, he could have come to find Marie and her siblings, and they could have regrouped together. But now it felt as though we were all taking our licks and not being given a chance to gain the upper hand. I could feel my frustration building.

"Damn it," I shouted, slamming my empty glass on the table. "What took you so long to get here, dude? Do you know how badly we struggled against just one of those freaks? And here you are with the cheat codes!"

Everyone fell silent. Marie's family looked at me as if I was going crazy, and heck, maybe I was. I could feel the alcoholic irrationality flowing through my veins. I felt like I needed to go home and sleep the whole night off, escape from my bitter mood. I felt so tired. Keith flew over to the edge of the bar and perched on a stool in front of me.

"Tyler, I'm sorry, but what the Wolf made me do is unforgivable. I made a vow to look like a creature of the forest until I find a way to bring them back. One day you, too, will have choices. I hope you make them wisely." I could feel the pain in Keith's words. Maybe I was being a jerk. He continued, "Tyler, listen. I may not be able to help you in battle, but this information on the Madonna could drastically improve your odds."

My eyes began to well up with tears; maybe there was hope after all.

"Sweets, my brother, and I had a little pow-wow with the one that calls himself the 'Flower.' No pun intended, but he planted our asses pretty well into the dirt." Marie drunkenly slurred.

Emily crossed her arms expectantly. "Well, Keith," she said, "Start talking. We clearly need the help."

"Very well, let's take it from the top," said the regal bird. "The one factor that can't be overlooked when mentioning the Madonna is their immense power. After all, they each were hand-picked by Daevas. However, they are not invincible. It pains me to say this, Tyler, but the Flower is the weakest of the bunch. Even so, he is extremely powerful. When you and Marie faced the Flower, I'm sure you noticed the tiara he wore on his head."

I could feel my face burning with embarrassment, but I pushed it down and nodded a reply.

"We noticed it, sure," agreed Marie, "But what does some stupid crown have to do with anything?"

"Maybe if you shut your trap, I could explain!" squawked Keith.

"Please, please, you guys, simmer down," Emily scolded. "Now, Keith, continue."

"Now, the tiara on the Flower's head is covered in many rare flowers, but it is one specifically that is his weakness. The Kadupul flower, better known as the Queen of the Night. The unique thing about this flower is that it typically blooms in the night, and wilts before dawn -- but not Flower's Kadupul. His is a storage facility for Flower's essence and acts as his literal heart and brain. It's actually quite ingenious: with the Kadupul hidden within his crown, Flower's body can take an immense amount of damage. Foes fall to him in battle because they cannot damage his two most vital organs."

"So, what you're saying is, squash the Kadupul, and you win," I said.

"You learn fast, Tyler," squawked Keith. "If I had a mouth instead of a beak, I'd smile approvingly."

"Wait, that's cool and all," Nicole chimed in, "But what about the other five Madonna? You said you knew all of their weaknesses."

Keith stretched out his wings, knocking over a bowl of bar nuts in the process. He quickly swooped to the edge of the bar where Nicole was sitting, digging his sharp black talons into the unpolished wooden countertop.

"That I do. Currently, two Madonna are on Terra with you: the Herculean and the Wolf. These are the two I encountered upon my arrival. Herculean is a massive hulking Angel with power to match his size. In order to sustain such massive bulk, his body has been modified with Angel cybernetics, powered by an interstellar energy generator. Herculean knows that this generator is his weak point and flying would expose its location underneath his wings. Destroy the generator, destroy Herculean."

"And the Wolf?" I asked.

"When it comes to the Wolf, I can't stress this enough to you all: do not let her touch you!"

"Let her touch you?" Preston joked, "Getting a little weird, huh, Keith?"

Keith lowered his sharp head in disapproval. "This is serious, you fool. What the Wolf lacks in sheer power, she makes up for in wit. The Wolf's main ability is not just copying the likeness of her opponents, but their power and abilities as well. This technique is called the Mimoto. The only way to prevent this is to get the Wolf's mask: get the mask and she can't steal anything from you."

I couldn't believe what I was hearing. This bird was pretty much giving us a cheat sheet for beating these guys. For the first time in months, I felt like we had a chance, a *real* chance.

"Okay Keith, that helps our problem so far, but what about the remaining three?" Emily had a knack for pointing out the obvious.

"You kids are so impatient," said Keith. "The next would be Torrid, 'of the flame,' I don't think I really need to explain his weakness."

"Why not?" asked McKenzie. The room grew silent, staring at McKenzie with bewilderment.

"You can't be serious?" Nicole screeched, "The word 'flame' is literally in his name!" Hurt, McKenzie burst into tears. Seriously, there was never a dull moment with these people.

"Even though Torrid's weakness is obvious," chirped Keith, "Don't snub his mastery of fire. The more frustrated he gets, the hotter the flames burn from the orb within his belly. It would be wise to make that a point of attack. Once he gets too enraged, his flames can get out of hand, making him much more difficult to fight."

Keith flew to the edge of the bar and began to peck peanuts out of a worn wooden bowl. "Now heed my warning," he said in between bites, "The final two Madonna are not to be trifled with."

"Maybe we can win this," Preston uttered with confidence, "I mean think about it, guys, our first encounter with a Madonna, he ambushed us. But now we have the inside track, and they're all on our turf, in smaller numbers!" He punctuated his statement by pounding his frothy beer mug onto the counter.

"You shut your teeth, boy," warned the bird, "You don't know how powerful Catacomb and Meridian are, turf or no turf! I can't stress this enough." I was feeling overwhelmed already, and stared into my beer mug, letting my vision blur into the white foam.

"Tyler, Tyler! You need to focus, this is important," Keith chided, snapping me to attention. "Catacomb is a master of the dream world. There is no real way to combat him in the waking world," said Keith. I looked up and struggled to focus on his words without letting my emotions overtake me, but I felt more and more out of control with each passing minute.

Oh god, how do I end up in these situations, why is Marie's family so loud ... my head is spinning. This is all too much.

"So how do we beat this guy?" Marie questioned.

Keith's face, even for a bird, said enough. "The only way to beat a dream lord is in a dream."

A dream, I thought, how the hell am I supposed to do that? I mean seriously, the last time I trained in the Usugurai I almost died fighting a nightmare. How do you beat a Dream Lord? "Dream" is literally in the guy's title! It's like the nonsense meter just gets higher and higher with this Angel and Demon crap!

"Okay Keith, what of the last one?" said Preston.

"Meridian. He is by far the most dangerous."

"And why is that? What's his deal?" McKenzie inquired. She had been quietly sulking since Nicole had made her cry, but it was clear that she was eating up the information as greedily as her siblings.

"His deal," Keith echoed. "He has the ability to exploit the flow of time."

"You mean he can stop time?" said Emily.

"No, more like he can actually control it. The only way to beat Meridian is to break the stream of time."

"What?!" I couldn't hold it in any longer. "Okay Keith, I'm willing to take a lot, but now you're asking me to somehow slip through time?" I felt like boiling water in a pot, overflowing with rage and uncertainty. "I mean Flowers, sure, weird Angel generators, sounds okay, power absorption, sign me up, and who doesn't love a good pyromaniac? But now? Now you're asking me to best a Freddy-Krueger-wannabe, and some nut that can control time?!" Before anyone could scold me or console me, I felt myself growing ill. "I need some air." Abruptly, I stood up and dashed outside.

As I stood on the corner, pushing down a panic attack, questions and fears raced through my mind. *How am I going to do this? What if I'm not the man I need to be in all of this? What about my family, how do I save them?* I heard the bar door swing open, momentarily carrying the noise of the jukebox and chattering voices outside. It swung shut and the night air was silent again but for the crickets and the steady click-clack of heels approaching behind me.

It was Emily.

"What's going on?" she asked gently.

"Honestly Em, I have no idea. This is all so much, I mean, you guys are like super-powered, I don't know... Demons. I'm just a regular guy who plays with computers, watches anime, and collects toys. You Demons have actual powers. Heck, even the talking bird is stronger than me. Sure, this mystical sword might help, but I don't know -- I'm just so...*normal.*"

While I was pouring my heart out, Emily stood quietly listening. When I was finished, she slowly took a sip of her light beer, deep in thought. She wiped a bit of foam off of her upper lip, the remnants of her red lipstick still hanging on after a night of carousing with her siblings.

"Ty, I get that this is a lot, and there's still so much that you don't fully understand. Nevertheless, you're trying. That means a lot to us, and even more to Marie and your children. Maybe in the thick of all of this, normal is what the universe needs right now. I know Empyrean could use a bit of normal. Keep your chin up."

With those words of wisdom, Emily gave me a hug for the second time that night. *Yep, she's definitely drunk,* I thought. She smelled like Chanel Number Five mixed with a hint of light beer, and I was now covered in glitter, again. But maybe she was right, maybe this crazy universe just needed a regular guy, someone *normal*, to balance the scales.

And who could be more normal than me?

VI
Our Little Secret

That's the last time I drink Empyrean acidulous lager, it's definitely not meant for humans. It was Monday, and I was still hungover. I struggled to maintain an upright position at my desk as I concentrated all my energy on not throwing up in the trash bin.

"Tyler, I need to see you in my office, now!"

Oh man, I thought. *What did I do now? How is it that I always end up in Natalie's talons?* I went to her office so much I should have set up a cot and a mini-fridge and just lived there. I took my usual seat and braced myself for the verbal beating.

"So, Tyler, I just wanted to say, excellent work on the computer lab upgrades! They look absolutely amazing." I supposed thanks were in order for the job well done, but that definitely wasn't my work. Oh well, she didn't need to know that.

"Ah, it was nothing Natalie, just doing my job." As I stood up to go, I was convinced Marie had to be behind this. I carefully walked out of Natalie's office, trying to not to wake the raging hangover that had been pounding in my skull since I had woken up. It had simmered down to a gentle thud-thud-thud, and I didn't want to anger it. I entered the empty bathroom and pressed Marie's speed-dial. *I know Marie did this, this has her name written all over it.*

"Hey sweets, what's up? I can't talk for long, it's busy in the hospital today." Her voice was dripping with joy. She loved nursing.

I turned the earpiece volume almost all the way down to keep the thudding headache to a minimum.

"Yeah, I get it. Just real quick: Did you use magic to, I don't know, finish my assignment at work?"

"Not me, sweets! So busy, gotta go, the sick and dying are waiting!" And with that the line went quiet.

Weird, if it wasn't Marie, then who? Certainly not my co-workers. I was pretty sure they would let me drown before lifting a finger to help me. I began to walk out of the restroom, then bam! I was in a dark room glowing in a purple hue. It reminded me of an amusement park funhouse -- disorienting walls that moved and flowed on their own terms.

"Hello?" I shouted, "Marie, is that you?" I couldn't detect the scent of mango. I knew the answer before it even came.

"Not even close," a voice replied.

"Who's there?" I shouted. "Preston, this isn't funny, man."

Nicole stepped out of the shadows in full demon form.

"Nicole, where are we? Why did you bring me here? Don't you have a guy to possess or something?"

Nicole laughed in my face, in her classic demeaning way. "Actually, dearest brother-in-law, you and I have work to do." I could tell by her grin that this undeniably meant vast amounts of danger. "So," she continued, not waiting for my response, "I've been doing some detective work and I stumbled upon something huge!"

"A shard!" I exclaimed excitedly. *God, I really need to work on my grown man voice, I sound like I'm auditioning for Rent.*

"Close, choir boy," Nicole replied. "I've found the location of the Tsuka."

"Tsuka? What the heck is that?" I swear it was always something new with these people.

"God, Tyler, you're so clueless. Tsuka is the hilt of Grus." Her tone made it sound as if she had asked what two plus two equaled and I had said green.

"Good to know," I said, "But why all the secrecy? Why not tell the others? What about Marie?" My stomach began to churn. I had the eerie feeling that I wasn't going to like what I was about to hear. That, or I needed to throw up again.

Nicole scoffed at me impatiently. "Look, do you want to help heal my dad or not?"

She could be such a bully. Of course, I wanted to help, but where was this going? "Here's the deal, Tyler. My father is in a coma, and quite honestly, it's going to take even more time to find the shards with the Madonna hot on our tails every time. And I have no faith in Keith. So, I've been working with a combination of Demon magic and smelting, I threw in a little Angel technology, and I think I was able to build a new sword. Part of it, anyway. It has the exact same properties, powers, and capabilities as the Sword of Grus. However, to power the blade, I require Grus' most important piece: Tsuka."

Interesting plan, I thought. "But Nicole, that's not part of the Three Deeds, is it? Is this even possible?" As the words tumbled out of my mouth, I regretted them. I felt a lecture in the air.

Nicole rolled her eyes. "Think of it like this, brother-in-law: when an archaeologist finds bones, odds are that not all of the bones are intact. So, in order to complete the skeletal structure, they often cast bones to replace the missing ones. I think I can perform a similar technique with the Sword of Grus."

I had to hand it to her, she was smart. Marie had told me that out of all of her siblings, Nicole was by far the best with alchemy and magic. And if this plan worked, it could speed up everything, including getting my life back to normal.

In my gut, I still felt a little skeptical, but she was staring at me expectantly, and I knew it would just be easier to go along. "Okay, Nicole, you've got a deal. Let's get the Tsuka and forge a sword.

"Also, thanks Nicole, for doing my work and making me look good! You're so smart and I'm not worthy of basking in your glory," said Nicole, mocking my voice while crossing her eyes and making a goofy face.

"I don't look like that!" I protested, then sheepishly added, "Thanks."

"Whatever, nerd," she said, already striding away from me. "Don't just stand there! Let's go!"

I came to find out that Nicole had already synthesized a new blade. All we required now was the hilt. I felt a headrush, thinking about what this could mean if we pulled it off. Marie's father would wake up, which meant he could finally put an end to those jerks, Camio and Loath. But what did it mean for Marie and the kids and me? I'm sure she would want to go back to Empyrean. I pictured myself living in a world with Demons and Angels, the only human for miles; no, light-years -- around. My stomach began to turn. But now was not the time to be selfish.

"Nicole, do you know the location of the Tsuka?" I was hoping she'd say something like, "Sure Tyler, it's right down the street."

"Wow Ty's, would you believe that it's actually right down the street!" shouted Nicole animatedly.

"Really?" I replied with a musical pitch.

"Ha," laughed Nicole, "I'm just busting your balls, I see why Marie picks on you."

Ugh, why do these Demons enjoy turning my mind into their personal playground?

Nicole analyzed her Windfall Stone. Her eyes began to glow

a bright red as if she were scanning the entire earth. "Okay, I've tracked the stone's location to a desert in Africa. Tyler, prepare for Wanderlust!"

Oh god, no, not the Wanderlust locket thing. I had totally forgotten about that. "On second thought, Nicole, umm, why don't you just go. I'm not much of a traveler, and besides, I get motion sickness."

"Don't be such a baby. God, I have no idea what Marie sees in you. Anyways, hold on!"

Before I could blink, we had landed somewhere else. I took a couple of steps away from Nicole, trying to regain my balance, and bent over double to throw up.

At least that's the last of the Demon lager, I thought, trying to be optimistic.

I stood up straight and Nicole was rolling her eyes at me. "Humans," she muttered.

We were in a vast African desert. There were sand dunes as far as the eye could see, and boy, was it hot. I mean, like, *hot* hot. I've always known it could get hot in Africa, but this was brutal. The sand blew past my face, carried on the wings of scorching air, and my mouth felt like a tennis ball. All I could think about was how long it had been since I had taken a sip of water.

Nicole's face lit up with glee as she looked around. It was as if this hunt for the Tsuka had somehow cured her boredom. As long as I had known her, she had always had an attitude. She was always salty or pissed about something or someone. But now that she was getting the opportunity to put her plan into effect she was glowing. Come to think of it, had I ever truly known Nicole?

"Hey Nicole, what part of Africa is this? The Namib? Kalahari?"

That's when she looked at me with a devious smile.

"This, brother-in-law, is the Pepo Desert."

The Pepo Desert? I had never seen this on a map, but then again, I'm terrible at geography. "How come I've never heard of this place, Nicole?"

"Simple," Nicole replied, "Because no human has ever made it out alive," and then she broke into a laugh. Yep, hysterical.

Great, it's always 'no human' this, 'no human' that with these guys. Man, it's hot here. If I had to guess, I would say it's at least 130 degrees. I'm shocked my skin hasn't begun to melt off of my face.

Nicole and I began to walk across the sands. We walked, and walked, and walked, and walked. I was so parched; all I could think about was water. That, and what Marie was going to do to me once she found out that I ran out with her sister to find a piece of this sword. I could only imagine. Ever since Marie had revealed to me that she was actually a Demon, it was like all bets were off. In recent weeks, any time I pissed Marie off she would turn the toilet paper into a bundle of snakes or make the bedroom walls bleed. Oh, and there was that time I called her crazy, and she turned me into a rat for a day. But never mind that, we were here on a mission -- a mission that could change everything.

Nicole and I approached a strange looking oasis. I felt like I had hit the lotto -- WATER, cool, clear, delicious water! Just one sip and I would be back in the game. I dropped to my knees and crawled as fast as I could to the pool, past a bush and a palm tree, as if I was a slave to it. I fixed my dry lips to take a sip, ready to experience heaven on earth.

That's when Nicole decided to smack me with a palm branch the size of a couch pillow.

"Ouch! Are you insane?" I screamed. A loaded question with this one. "What the heck was that for?"

Nicole looked at me as if I flunked a two-question quiz. "Don't be stupid, Tyler, the water in this desert is pure poison, toxic mineral water. One lick and I'd be dragging your body home to Marie in a bag." How the heck was I supposed to know that? She continued to berate me, but I found I had to strain to hear her. Her voice was being drowned out by something. The winds? The sand whipping around us? I glanced around. The hot air was annoyingly still. Not even a breeze, cool or not. So, what was happening? Gradually the muddled noises in my head began to clear. I could hear beautiful singing, just like the time at Sakura. I slowly placed my hand in the water.

"Tyler!" Nicole screamed, interrupting her diatribe. "Don't you listen? What the hell do you think you're doing?"

"I...I don't know, but I think this water is calling out to me," I replied.

As if in a trance, I plunged my hand deep into the mineral water. Strange. I could see the pink steam emitting off of my skin, I could feel heat, but felt no pain. It was like being outside of my body and deeper inside of it than I had ever been at the same time. My heart rate began to slow, I was pouring sweat, my mouth began to water – there's some irony for you.

Swishing and swirling my hand around in the murky depths I stumbled upon what I thought was a stone. My fingers explored the length of it, and I broke into a smile. This had to be the Tsuka!

I pulled the hilt from the spring and it began to shake in the palm of my hand. The crusty exterior cracked and fragmented, revealing a design of sheer beauty. A silver hilt etched with gold; a weapon fit for a king.

Too bad I was just good ol' Tyler Pine.

I turned to look at Nicole. Her mouth was practically watering with desire. She placed her hands together as if starting to pray, then closed her eyes and began to chant. As she slowly pulled her hands apart, a shiny blade appeared. A blade that was perfect in every way -- I'm no blade expert, but even I could tell this was a powerful weapon. Yellow electricity was popping off of the saber like hot grease in a skillet.

"Tyler, hand me the Tsuka," Nicole said.

I was frozen in disbelief. She had done it. She recreated this so-called sword of legend.

"Now, Tyler; we don't have much time."

As unsure as I had been about this plan, I didn't hesitate to pass the Tsuka to Nicole. Nicole grabbed it out of my hands and placed the blade into the Tsuka, then reached into the breast of her shirt and re-moved what appeared to be a fuchi collar for the sword. She placed it on the base of the sword and raised it up to test it. But as quickly as the power and energy had come into the blade, it subsided. The blade went dark. It looked like an ordinary sword.

Nicole's face fell in confusion and despair.

"What's happening? I...I don't understand. Why is this blade los-ing its power?!" Nicole screamed.

All I could think about were the stories I had heard about me, the Merozantine, the Sword, my ancestors. These thoughts were swirl-ing around in my head like finely mixed pancake batter. Was it truly meant for my hand alone?

A burst of light cracked through the hot desert sky. A great, blinding white ray scorched the ground of the oasis, turning the sands as black as fresh coal. Soot filled the air and began to fill my lungs like cold air in the middle of January. Through a coughing fit, I managed to croak, "What the heck is going on?"

But I couldn't see Nicole. I couldn't see the sword, either. I could feel the earth rumbling beneath my feet, as a rhythmic stomping om-inously filled the air. Whoever or whatever it was stepped through the smoke and stopped in front of me.

I raised my head in disbelief. Before me was a massive hulking man, his body engraved with what appeared to be wires and tubes. The wings on his back were far greater than any bird I'd ever seen.

"Nicole, Nicole!" I shouted in a panic, not taking my eyes off the creature. "Where are you? Are you okay?"

The hulking man dropped to one knee and looked me in the face, his eyes cold and glowing. His glare sent an icy chill down my spine.

"Scanning complete, target acquired," the Angel spoke in a robotic voice. "I would not concern myself with your compatriot. I will only ask once, please release any shards in your possession. And I will guarantee a quick disposal."

Quick disposal? This has to be a Madonna, no doubt about it.

I quickly ran for cover behind a smattering of broken palm trees. Where was Nicole, did she give me the slip? She wouldn't try to keep the sword for herself, would she? No, not a chance – she knew the importance of family. She was here somewhere. I had to find her. I slowly poked out my head, seeking a safe path.

I guess this is how ants feel when a boot is nearby. If I stay here too long, this guy is going to beat me like I stole his lunch.

I had to make a break for it.

As I was running from the creature's pursuit, it began to launch a series of attacks in my direction. I scrambled as fast as I could to avoid getting hit. I knew I would have to face him sooner or later, and summoning Sardna seemed like my best bet. Then I heard a faint voice near a pile of trees. It was Nicole! She was injured, covered in soot – she must have been hit by this jerk's grand entrance.

"Nicole, are you okay? Can you walk? " I was starting to panic; last time I faced a Madonna, Marie saved me. I couldn't do this without help.

"I...I can, but Tyler, we won't get far. You need to end this."

Nicole passed me the newly forged sword. I knew what time it was. As soon as the Tsuka touched my palm, it began to glow a bright purple. Yellow sparks of light began to crackle up and down the sword. The sound reminded me of popcorn cooking in a kettle. I could feel its power coursing through my arm. All this time I thought the Sardna was powerful, but this was unbelievable! I was bursting with confidence; I felt like I could take on the world. *This must be what jocks felt like before the big game.* I could feel my senses slowly enhancing, and my muscles starting to tighten. I turned to the Angel.

"Okay Madonna, we enjoyed your flashy entrance. But the show's over!" Maybe it was the sword, but I could feel myself growing bold.

The creature's eyes began to flicker. "Scanning complete: you would be correct in your analysis. I am the one they call the Herculean, the fourth strongest Beast of the Madonna." The creature wasted no time with his assault. He dashed toward me, leading with a punch.

My god, I thought. *Look at this freak! His fist alone is the size of a Volkswagen, maybe I'm in over my head. But this time something seems different. It's like the sword is taking control of my body.*

I threw up my blade in a defensive stance and blocked the Herculean's punch, the contact of the blade and his mighty fist cutting the earth's surface like Nazca lines. Somehow, I had managed to absorb the punch. That's when I remembered what Keith had told us that night in the bar: every Beast has a weakness.

That's it, I'll get him to leave the ground!

I ran towards the beast with my sword drawn. I could tell he was squaring up for another punch. I was running faster than I had ever run, and I had to time this just right. At the very last second before he could attack, I used my blade as a pole vault and launched myself into the air. I had to be at least a hundred feet off of the ground. Surprising myself further, I momentarily stopped in midair. This definitely was the sword's power at work. I fell back to the earth, hurtling at the monster, preparing to slash the beast with everything I had.

As I plummeted toward the earth, I heard a distinctive sound -- *vashhhh, ziiiip* – he was opening his mechanical wings. That generator thing Keith spoke of would be exposed. If I could bounce back up once he was in the air maybe I could smash it – with an attack from below. The Herculean left the ground at rocket-like speeds.

Just a bit higher, I thought. *Then I'll make my move.*

Then the unthinkable happened: while in the air, the Herculean's shoulders opened up, exposing some sort of biomechanical missile launcher. I was speechless. I didn't count on this happening. In mere seconds, two Angelic tech missiles were heading in my direction.

"Targeting complete. Probability of subject escape zero, mission success rate 80% and climbing," the Herculean monotoned.

"Oh god, I don't think I can avoid those," I mumbled.

I was able to deflect one of the missiles, but the other clipped my shoulder and sent me plummeting into the sand. I was hurting, and I had definitely broken a few bones. To make matters worse, I was badly bleeding. I tried to crawl, but the pain was too intense.

"Ahhh, oh God this...this hurts so bad! Oh God, oh no," I glanced down to my ribs to see a piece of metal protruding from my side. I started to shiver uncontrollably. I would have given anything for Marie in that moment; she would know what to do.

How stupid of me, thinking that a shortcut like making a new sword would just solve my problems. Classic me, I guess, always looking for the easy way out, the loophole.

Everything was getting fuzzy; blood was in my eyes. I heard the massive footsteps of my executioner. *Marie, I really do love you, please take care of those children.* Everything was starting to go black. A puff of purple smoke surrounded me. It was Nicole.

"Tyler...Tyler...hang on, brother. I'm going to fix this."

Before I could gather enough air to respond we were on the other side of the oasis. Nicole sat me under the last intact palm tree.

"Hang in there, Tyler. Shit, the healing magic isn't working. Your wound...this damn wound is too deep!" Her voice was sounding quieter and quieter, like she was retreating down a dark tunnel.

"Tyler...Tyler, you ass. Stay with me, oh God..."

Through my pain, I strained to hear her. I thought I was making my lips move, but my throat wouldn't push out any sounds.

"Oh Tyler, please, please, please-please-please, don't do this. Marie will never forgive me for this. Okay, hold on, hold on, I...I have an idea. I just hope it's not too..." I descended into a black fog and her voice faded until there was only silence.

My body, my mind, were perfectly numb. I couldn't feel anything. A few sparse memories flitted through my head. I tried to remember my name.

And then, a blinding, searing pain. My collarbone was on fire. A white light blinded my eyes.

"What the, what!" I screamed, sitting up. "I felt like I was dead. No, I'm positive I was. What just happened? And umm, Nicole, why are you biting me?" My sister-in-law had her head buried between my shoulder and my neck. The scent of ash and sweat slowly crept to my nostrils. I had a little of Nicole's long black hair caught in my mouth. As I tried to blow it away, I could feel her breath beating on my neck. What exactly was going on here?

Nicole sat back and wiped her lip. A trickle of deep purple liquid had been smeared across her chin. Her face lit up with joy. "Thank goodness you're alive."

I looked at Nicole with puzzlement, "What the heck happened, I just remember being hit by...THAT BEAST! Where is it?!" I shouted.

"Shh, keep your voice down. Look, I think I got us a good distance away, but he's definitely going to catch up. Now Tyler, what I'm about to tell you is very important. You have to promise me that you will never bring this up ever again."

I could tell by the look on Nicole's face that this was serious, maybe even more so than the Madonna that was currently hunting us.

"No worries, Nicole, I...I won't say anything." I braced myself for the news.

"Very well," mumbled Nicole. "I know this isn't going to be easy for you to hear, Tyler. But due to your injuries, you died just a few moments ago."

Wait, what did she say? No way. "Are you sure about that? If so, how in the world am I talking to you?"

"Tyler, just listen, you idiot. Yes, you died, you bit the big one! The hit you took, the wound was far too deep, and too much time had passed for me to use healing magic. That being the case, I had to inject you with Demonic Blood. It was the only way to get you back, to save your life."

I blinked, taking it all in. Nicole bit her lip nervously, and concluded: "So, in a nutshell, you're now a Transient with Demon blood sustaining you."

This couldn't be real; it was a sick joke. I felt like I was going to puke. Did this make me a Demon? But I was a human, I didn't want this.

"You're lying, Nicole! I don't believe you, I just don't."

Deep down, I knew she was telling the truth. Hell, I could already feel the changes. I already missed what it felt like to be my old self.

"Ty, it's the truth. I had to save you. Besides, I didn't have the heart to tell Marie that I'm responsible for her husband's death. And, I have a small confession to make." She paused and lowered her eyes. "I had every intention of keeping Grus for myself, I didn't trust that you would be able to help us or wield its power. I was wrong, but actually right, too, at the same time."

Classic Nicole, I thought. *Way to take ownership.*

"I now see, Tyler, it's true we need you for the Three Deeds, and only you can wield Grus. The blood of the Merozantine flows strong in you, but it's also true that you were far too weak, and eventually you would have died one way or another. You're just a human, and humans are fragile."

I couldn't believe what I was hearing. I didn't know whether to feel loved or insulted. Too weak, yeah, that sounds about right. I mean seriously, where did I think this was going to go? I'd been lucky, but that was bound to run out at some point, right?

"So why must this all remain a secret?"

Nicole's face looked guilty, but I believed her intentions had to be good.

"In our world it is forbidden to indulge in any consumption of Demonic or Angelic Blood. It is always to remain pure. If anyone finds out about this, it means instant banishment from Empyrean. If Marie finds out she won't tell a soul, but if the Grand Synod got wind of it, she would be banished as well, just for knowing. So, you see, Tyler, you can never speak of this, EVER." Her eyes were insistent, and full of something I had never seen in her before: fear. "When you're around Marie or any of my other siblings, try your hardest to suppress your new Demonic traits."

Keeping secrets from Marie? Ugh, that's like Ruin Your Marriage 101. Especially when it came to a secret as big as this. But what choice did I have? It could ruin everything if I flapped my gums. I knew how important it was to wake their father, and how much they wanted to return to Empyrean. I could never take any of that away.

The sun was burning my face. It was hot and I was getting uncomfortable again. Fitting conditions to absorb this bombshell of information.

"Okay Nicole, I get it; this secret is safe with me."

"Perfect, Ty, but now's not the time to have an in-law bonding moment. It looks like our tall stupid-looking friend with the muscles and laser missiles is back. I think it's time for you to test your new blood with that shiny sword."

I rose to my feet and grabbed Grus from the scorched sand. I took a deep breath. My mind was racing.

Okay, I can do this. It's time for a rematch, and it's time to end this. I'm so sick of these bullies; it's always bullies, ever since elementary school. Well, today it stops! Today, just try *to bully me.*

I could feel my teeth becoming sharp, my body starting to gain bulk and muscle. I looked at my reflection in the shiny blade. My pupils were now purple. There was no mistake, I was a Demon. But not like Nicole, not like Preston, and not like Marie. I could still feel the essence of my humanity.

I guess this is what an electric car feels like, running on a different source of fuel, but at its core still a car._

STOMP, STOMP, STOMP. It was the Herculean approaching.

"Scanning complete...subjects located. Your efforts to hide are futile, brace yourself for combat," grumbled the Herculean in his mechanical voice.

He threw the first blow with his fist, and I dodged it effortlessly. His shoulders opened for a second missile blast. *Not this time,* I thought.

I dodged and dodged again, evading the Herculean missiles, forcing them to crash into one another. I was moving so fast, it was exhilarating!

Am I crazy, or is he having trouble tracking my movements?

As though it was second nature for me, I dashed past the Madonna in a dizzying burst of speed. I didn't think I could move that fast! I was moving at what felt like a Mach Three. I reappeared behind the monster.

"Systems unable to track target, recalculating...recalculating...recalculating." I could see the Herculean was becoming frustrated. I had the upper hand. I was winning--and I was angry. This was an anger that I had never felt before. It was pure rage, bubbling inside of me. And I was going to take it out on this beast.

"What's wrong, having trouble tracking me? I can see by your face that all of those hi-tech enhancements didn't remove fear." This wasn't me; I've never been this confident or cocky – at least not out loud. "And guess what, big boy, today you die!" I laughed triumphantly.

Wait, die? Did I just say die? I'm not that kind of person. No matter how bad this creature is, does he deserve to die? My inner thoughts were conflicting with what was coming out of my mouth. *No, no, no, I'm no killer!* I could feel my human side pleading with my demon side. I couldn't believe that my body and mind weren't getting along.

"So long, Madonna, the scrap pile is waiting!" With a wild grin, I jumped on the Herculean's back and grabbed one of his wings in each of my hands. I ripped both of the wings clean from his shoulder blades. It was like ripping pages out of a book. I landed on the ground and threw the wings down with an ear-splitting crash.

"What have you done!" screamed the Herculean. "Get...you have no idea what...you're...you're doing." The creature's back was crackling and popping as his voice slowed down. The lights in his eyes were blinking out of sync. He was beginning to malfunction.

From where I stood, I could see Herculean's generator fully exposed. I flipped Grus around in my hand with an acrobatic twirl and jammed it into the generator.

"No, don't, noooo...!" screamed the Herculean, his mechanical voice lowering in pitch until it seemed to ooze out of him in a low moan. The creature began to spark like foil in a microwave, eventually exploding, generating a mushroom cloud of mammoth proportion.

A great blast rang throughout the oasis, the palm trees carried away in the gust. I glanced to my left and saw Nicole covering her face from the tailwinds of the explosion.

The smoke began to clear, revealing pieces of the Herculean scattered about the now devastated oasis. Nicole was covered in sand, soot and mechanical goo. On her face was a mix of excitement and fear.

Fear. I didn't like being the cause of that look. I wasn't in control, but the Demonic side of me was. I stood amid the rubble, clutching Grus in my palm. The Tsuka was immaculate, but the blade that Nicole had created was riddled with cracks. We both watched as the blade burst into dust and was carried away with the dry desert wind.

I guess at the end of it all, there is no shortcut. Nicole and I sat in the remnants of the oasis as I slowly reverted back to my normal human-looking self.

"Hell of a ride, huh, Ty?" Nicole threw her arm around my neck and gave me a noogie as if I were her kid brother. "You did good, Ty. Just remember that this is our little secret. No one needs to know about the Demon blood I placed in your bloodstream. Also, get those powers in check; we'll need them if we want the last two shards."

"Aren't you upset about the sword, Nicole?"

"Nope, not really, killer! Let's get you home and report this to the others. And if they ask, just say *I* found a way to kill that Madonna."

Nicole used her Wanderlust locket to open a portal home. "Ready, killer?" she repeated my new nickname with a playful jab in my ribs.

"Yeah right, 'killer,'" I murmured to myself. And yet I felt myself rebelling against my new identity. I wouldn't let something as clinical as a blood transfusion redefine who I was.

Who cares if I have Demon blood coursing through my veins? I'm a human. Normal old Tyler Pine. And like Emily said, maybe normal is what the universe needs.

Interlude
Shah Mat

Lonely and dispirited, King Araqiel sat in his cell deep in the realm known as Damabiath. It had been quite some time since another soul had visited.

Every year during the rise of the Enceladus moon, Camio would come to see the fallen King and engage him in a chess match. The former friends, now foes, stimulated their minds with a game of wit. It was a tense interaction, but one that kept the King's spirits alive and his mind sharp. As much as he despised the Demon for his betrayal, the presence of another living being kept his hope alive that one day he could again see the world beyond his bars.

However, wise King Araqiel had a different visitor on this day, seeking more than hypothetical strategy across a grid of squares.

"Who goes there? State your purpose," commanded the King, his voice hoarse with disuse. "Show yourself." He had lost so much while in captivity, but his presence had not diminished. There was no fear in his tone.

A voice came out of the darkness, soft and sinister. "Is that any way to greet a former ally?"

"Wolf... by the Old Gods' light, is that you?" The King rubbed his eyes as if they deceived him. His robes were tattered and filthy with dirt, and grime infested his large hands. The scent of excrement wafted through the cell.

"My goodness. It's been ages; simply seeing you reminds me of my early days as King. Fighting the Grootslang together and protecting the kingdom, blades in hand. Those were glorious times!" He paused, mired in nostalgia. A faint smile played across his lips. "I would think Camio would accompany you; nevertheless, I shall not complain. I don't receive many visitors in this God-forsaken place. I must admit, I'm quite shocked to see you setting foot in such squalor."

The Wolf raised her porcelain-colored hands, removing the battle-worn wolf skull that covered her beautiful pale face. Her cold gray eyes emerged, glaring deep into the soul of the former king.

"I've never been one to shy away from getting my hands dirty. You above anyone else should know this," said the Wolf as she swept away the white hair that fell into her eyes.

"Yes, how foolish of me," said the King. "This hell hole erodes one's memory. I had always hoped for a warrior's end. The blaze of battle, in the jaws of a Grootslang. Yet here I am, closer to a beast than a man. Rotting away, a far cry from my former life."

The Wolf's pale face cracked a menacing smile, "Former life," she chuckled as she rubbed the scar covering her eye. "Indeed, we've seen a lot together." She raised her porcelain hand, polishing her manicured claws on her snow-white fleece. "Araqiel..." murmured the Wolf, as she analyzed her sharp black nails. "Do you know what they say my weakness is?"

The King set down the pot from which he had been drinking stagnant water, droplets suspended in his scraggly beard. He fixed his eyes on the Wolf, who slowly scanned the King from head to toe. She had begun to pace the damp cell, circling like a shark. Her eyes locked on his.

"They say I'm number three of the Madonna. I'm not really sure who makes these ranks, perhaps you could enlighten me, oh wise king," said the Wolf sarcastically. "The people of this kingdom believe what they want; even a fly-on-the-wall testimony wouldn't be enough to change their minds. They call the Madonna monsters; they say my powers only come from those I drain. I've also heard them say that my powers stem solely from this mask. It's insulting."

"What is this all about, Wolf?" Araqiel demanded, puzzled by her monologue.

"Have you ever heard of the Seraphs?" asked the Wolf.

"Do you test the vastness of my intelligence? I am more than familiar; one does not rule a kingdom without having knowledge of all of its inhabitants, past and present. The Seraphs were The Gods' of Old most favored Angels."

"But do you know of our great curse?" replied the Wolf.

"Whatever do you mean," questioned Araqiel.

"You see, Araqiel, there is only one Seraph born every two millennia. With the birth of one Seraph brings the death of another. Only one can exist in time. From birth we are abused: used as tools in a quest for power and energy, forced into battle with the Grootslang. Yet, if I steal anything without my superior's orders, I would be a castaway. With the abilities that I possess and the proper host, I could achieve powers greater than any Seraph before me. Araqiel looked at the Wolf with concern. He wondered where this soliloquy was leading.

"Wolf, tell me: what is your endgame?"

"I'm glad you're listening, Araqiel; my endgame is simple. I wish to be a God."

"A God... A Being of Old. No one, not even I, could achieve power on that level. Trust me, to even seek it is insanity."

"Which brings me to my next point," smirked the Wolf. She

reached into her fleece and removed the small holo-chip recovered from the body of the Herculean.

"I think this footage will interest you," she said. "I recovered this from our former compatriot, Herculean."

"Former... recovered? Surely you jest, Wolf!"

"The Herculean has been destroyed. Slain at the hands of a Merozantine. Well, with a bit of assistance, of course."

The king began pacing erratically throughout his cell, slamming his fist into the moist stone wall.

"Transformed or not, he was once good. He was a friend, a brother in arms!" wept the king. He fell to his knees, splashing into a puddle of grimy water. "We Angels and Demons take for granted our long lives, often losing sight of the possibility of death. Ignoring the fact that we, too, are susceptible to illness and injury," said Araqiel, clenching and unclenching his hand, musing over the blood on his fist.

The Wolf activated the holo-chip and replayed the Herculean footage. Nicole's voice echoed in the prison chamber, crackling and tinny. *"Just remember our little secret. No one needs to know about the Demon Blood I placed in your bloodstream..."*

"That's...one of Daevas' children. Nicole, if I'm not mistaken. What in Empyrean's name is she doing with a Merozantine?" Araqiel inquired.

"As fate would have it, Marie, the middle child of Daevas, married into the Merozantine bloodline in an attempt to lift the curse of the deeds. It was a ploy to save her father," said the Wolf in a derisive tone.

"And what in the world does this have to do with me?" asked Araqiel.

"Don't play coy with me," the Wolf said, once again circling the distraught King. "I know that your sister was the love of Daevas' life. And you wished to honor her final request. Helping Daevas move forward, seeing his family taken care of. But have you ever told him the truth after all of these years? Her illness, and how you caused it? Pushing her harder, and harder to unlock the secrets of Old Magic. All for the sake of your precious Transient experiment, totally oblivious to the harm it was causing her. You have promises to keep, do you not?"

Araqiel lowered his head in shame. "Yet here I am, reduced to this life. It's my fault, Wolf. I should have done something the day Merozantine invaded the castle! I should have believed Daevas," wept the King.

"Which brings me to my next juncture. To become a God, I require more power. And I have found a way to ascend to such a level."

The King continued to weep silently.

The Wolf continued, "You will fuse with me. You will undergo the Dark Mutatio with me as the main host!"

"Are you mad!" shouted Araqiel through his tears. "I will do no such thing. Two Angels' powers combined in one body would be an abomination! There is no way we would survive it."

The Wolf began to laugh. "How easy you forget. I am of the Seraph race. I was meant to absorb. This is my destiny."

"Destiny or not, I will not comply with this!" shouted the King.

"Is that so?" the Wolf replied sternly. "Then perhaps I'll just surrender this footage to Loath. You well know the punishment for the mingling of Blood without consent. Or maybe you prefer letting your friend and your beloved sister down for a second time."

Araqiel knew he had no choice. He may have been living in a cell, but in his mind, he was still a King, and Kings must undertake the most difficult choices. But as in chess, every move has a purpose.

"Well played, Wolf." He paused. "However, if I am to make this sacrifice you must promise me one thing."

"I don't think you're in a position to make a plea," replied the Wolf.

"Not even for the man that saved your life?" Araqiel replied. "Or have you forgotten? How you were moments from being destroyed by the Grootslang, and I risked my life because I knew," the King looked into the Wolf's eyes, "I *knew* how special you were."

As her eyes flickered with remembrance, the Wolf's hand automatically came to her face, touching the raised white scar. She jerked her hand away and replaced her mask. The scar was a continual reminder of the day she let her guard down. She couldn't deny Araqiel.

"Very well...Speak!" said the Wolf begrudgingly.

"You must help Daevas and his children. I made a promise long ago. As much as it galls me, I can't uphold that oath from a cell. But you can bring them justice. Bring them home. Do this for me, Wolf, and I'll give you omnipotence." Araqiel would not let the Ashi family name go down in flames.

The Wolf knew that a plan of this magnitude would have to be carefully calculated. If caught, she would face treason charges followed by execution. In order to achieve her goal, she must first disappear. It must be authentic and feel as final as death.

She returned to the one place Angels and Demons alike feared the most: The Outskirts of Empyrean, beyond the safety of the kingdom's grand walls. The Outskirts were nothing more than a wilderness, a vast plain consisting of the harshest elements, from frozen tundra to smoldering jungle. This was the lair of the Grootslang.

She wasted no time pursuing her quarry. The Grootslang she found was young and inexperienced but managed to keep her at bay. Even so, the Wolf used her unrivaled wit and power to capture the beast.

With the Grootslang now in hand, the pieces were not yet set into play. Long ago, the Wolf acquired an ancient relic, The Living Armor of Alloces. Alloces wasn't much of a monster; he was a lesser Demon and one of Araqiel's earliest foes, but his armor's power was brilliant. Upon his defeat the Wolf kept the armor, and now wished to trap the soul of a Grootslang within.

Once trapped, the monster could only obey the owner of the armor. It was the perfect way to help Daevas' family without getting caught by Loath or Camio. However, that still left her in servitude to Loath. But one could not serve if they were presumed dead.

VII
Don't Be Shy

"Tyler, DUCK!" screamed Preston, as he smacked away one of Torrid's minions.

Here we go again, another day in the life. I guess on the bright side of things, I'm getting to travel a bit.

It had been three weeks since my battle with the Herculean. We had managed to track down the third shard. Nothing too crazy – it was just hanging out, practically at the bottom of the ocean off the coast of Auckland, New Zealand. Luckily, Nicole had cooked up some magic to help us breath underwater, but I was so tired. We had gotten off to an early start this morning, and I couldn't wait to just get back to the hotel and sleep. The sun was barely up, and the fog rolling off the water was as thick as Marie's homemade chili. And to top it off, it was raining – we were simultaneously getting pelted by fire and water. Some vacation.

"What the heck are these things, Preston?" I shouted. "It seems like this Torrid dude has an endless supply of them."

"They're called Flame Dancers," Preston replied, as he smashed one of the creatures beneath his morning star. "Another form of a Pooka. They're not all that strong. But because they love heat, they adore Torrid. They also have great numbers."

Madonna, flames, monsters—heck, anymore, it seemed like a game of the Price is Right minus Bob Barker. I might as well have spun a wheel. Yet it seemed Marie, Nicole, and Emily had a good hold on our new contestant. As a fire demon, Torrid's weakness was fairly simple. The combination of Marie's wind magic, Emily's ability to manipulate water, and Nicole's knowledge of alchemy was giving this guy a world of hurt, quite literally raining on his parade. Torrid was different from the other Madonna I had encountered. He seemed to be more of an actual beast. He even looked like one: he was red in color, with a slender build that reminded me of a newt or salamander, except he walked upright. His body was covered in shiny silver armor containing a glowing hot orb in the center of his stomach. His skin was smoldering to the touch, with each drop of misty rain turning to steam upon contact. Unlike the other Madonna, Torrid did not fight with tactic or skill. Instead, he seemed to function on pure rage.

"Enough of this nonsense!" grumbled Torrid, "You will all burn! This is for the glory of the Madonna! I will have your heads as well as your shards!"

"Shut your damn mouth, you stupid lizard!" shouted Marie as she kicked Torrid clean in the neck.

Torrid began to glow a bright red. He was overwhelmed with frustration from the constant onslaught of Marie and Emily's magic. We *all* had become a lot stronger, and more importantly, thanks to Keith, we were functioning as a team.

"Emily! Marie! Focus your attacks on his core! Nicole, use a potion on them to boost their powers!" chirped Keith as he swooped over the battlefield. He was amazing, like a little fighter jet or something, barrel-rolling in between the maelstrom of flames Torrid was spewing. It was nice to have him as our coach.

"That's it, you brats," screamed Torrid, "If I can't have the shards, then neither can you! I'll self-destruct right here, in the middle of this city!"

Marie furiously dashed past Preston and me. She cast a Gale Spell out of the palm of her hand, summoning a powerful tornado which whistled with lightning, aiming it at Torrid. It was a direct hit. Emily followed up with a barrage of water spells, spraying the Torrid with firehose-like pressure. With the final attack, Nicole's frost bomb, Torrid was literally frozen in his tracks.

I cautiously approached the Demon and touched his icy shell. He felt like February in the middle of a forest. His eyes, which I could just make out through the smooth ice, were cold and lifeless. Torrid slowly began to crack, finally bursting into a million tiny snowflakes, which blew away with the breeze. I felt the prickle of ice on my skin as a series of goosebumps formed below my rolled-up sleeve. I'd never seen ice or wind magic. Marie had explained it to me a little bit, but wow, it was even more impressive in person. I kneeled next to a pile of snow, a leftover from the spell, and scooped it into my warm hands.

I couldn't believe we had won! No casualties, no crazy Demon blood transfusions, just a win for the good guys. The streets of Auckland were now barren, all that was missing was a rolling tumbleweed. Our ruckus had scared everyone away. Or at least, that's what we thought.

"Bravo!" shouted a voice whipping eerily through the air. "It would seem you all have increased your strength tremendously." We turned to see a tall figure emerging from the patch of dense fog. "I never really cared for Torrid. Such a clumsy beast, nothing more than a brawler. If it weren't for his mastery of fire, the King would have stripped him of his rank ages ago. And, no pun intended, he was a bit of a hothead." We could hear the figure grin under the full mask she wore, a momentary glimmer of emotion. "I would savor this brief moment of victory. You've managed to beat yet another

Madonna. On your own, too. You didn't even have to rely on stolen Demon gifts."

Oh no, I thought. *How does this person know about my new powers?* I looked over at Nicole. Her face was ghost white; she looked as if she was going to vomit. If this person knew about our secret, we were in big trouble.

"Shut your mouth, lady!" Marie screamed. "You're just mad we've gotten stronger, and now we have your number. So, if you're through, come out here and fight already!"

As the fog slowly dissipated, rolling off to the ocean waters nearby, we were able to catch a better glimpse of this new adversary. The Wolf. Keith gracefully landed on a light post above me, looking nervous.

I didn't know birds could sweat, I thought.

"Tyler, be careful," he said, "This Madonna isn't like anything you've faced thus far."

The fact that she knew my secret made me feel like she had already beaten me. I could tell that Nicole was shaken as well. This was a mental game to her. If this had been chess, this Wolf lady had a Fool's Mate on us from the moment she walked in.

I glanced furtively at Marie to see if she was trying to put two and two together. The last thing we needed was a big spousal argument, right here, in the middle of our mission. I imagined Marie would do more than turn me into a rat this time. Things weren't looking good.

"You." The Wolf calmly pointed in my direction. I could feel the blood stopping in my veins.

Don't say it.

"You haven't shared your little secret with your family, have you? Don't be shy, I'm sure everyone here is dying to know."

Nicole's face was practically stone. *This is it,* I thought, *Nicole is going to hurl.*

"What are you babbling about, lady? You don't know my sweets," said Marie, clenching her fists. "Leave him alone!"

"Sweets?" the Wolf mused, "Oh, I see, now this is truly interesting. You're the Demon wife? Well, then. I suppose you should be made aware that your 'sweets' is not who he appears to be."

Marie's brows furrowed in confusion and anger. "What in the world are you talking about?"

"Even if you get the shards, and restore your father, you're not going back to Empyrean. You will all be banished." She chuckled beneath her mask.

"Banished! On what grounds?" asked Preston.

"On the grounds of being accomplices to illegal Toxin transfusion! Isn't that right, Nicole?"

"Nicole, what the hell is going on?" asked Marie.

Nicole's eyes filled with tears and her words came tumbling out in a rush.

"Look, Marie, I swear I had no choice. Tyler and I went after the shard, and he was dying. I...I didn't want to, but I couldn't just let him die."

Marie was silent, but I didn't need to be married to her for the last seven years to see that she was bubbling over with rage. She fixed her sister with a look of pure wrath.

"Marie, please, it wasn't just Nicole. It was my fault as well. We were desperate, so we figured we would try to just make a new Grus. Things didn't go as planned and that Madonna attacked us. I should have told you."

I could tell that Marie wasn't hearing anything I was saying. She was pissed, and I couldn't even tell her she was overreacting. She had every right to be angry.

"Figures as much. Not thinking. You *never* think, Nicole! You always have to be right; it's your way or nothing at all! And now you've ruined *everything!*"

I had to say something. "Marie, she was just trying to help is all, I don't think..."

"Shut it, Tyler!" Marie snapped. "You're not exempt from this either. I can't believe you would keep something like this from me. Do you have any idea of the implications this could have? How long ago did this happen?"

I lowered my head in shame. "Marie, is this necessary?"

"How long ago, Tyler!" Marie screamed.

"About three weeks ago," I admitted reluctantly.

At those words, Marie lost it. She transformed into her Max Power. Back was the fiery red mane, an odd pattern of runes all over her skin, and her medallion was glowing and fused to her chest. Her wings had large claws protruding out of them. Silver gauntlets, with sharp metal wings, appeared around her forearms. "God, she's so hot like this," I drooled, momentarily forgetting that I was the object of her rage.

"Tyler!" screamed Nicole, "Stop being a perv and get your head in the game."

Right, we had to get Marie back to normal. "Hey, Nicole, can you change forms like that? I mean, I'm sure the two of you can take on one Madonna."

"Of course, I can, you moron; we all can. But it's not safe, using a form like that can kill you. It only happens to Marie because she can't control her temper." Why did this information not surprise me? I remembered of the bundle of snakes on my toilet paper roll.

Unable to direct her anger at me and her sister, Marie dashed towards the Wolf in a flash, grabbing her by the throat and slamming her into a building. She repeatedly bashed Wolf's head into the wall. Placing her hand over her mask, Marie shouted, "I don't like this stupid thing! I wanna see your face just before I kick your ass!"

Marie ripped Wolf's mask from her face and crushed it in the palm of her hand.

"Looks like Halloween's over," said Marie sarcastically, "As well as your powers."

It seemed as though Marie had the upper hand. Yet I couldn't shake the feeling that things were about to get worse.

"Silly child," chuckled the Wolf. "I see that imbecilic rumor spread like wildfire. Imagine: that my power could be destroyed by eliminating a simple mask. That mask was just to cover a scar from my past, nothing more."

The Wolf grabbed Marie's wrist and wrenched it behind her back, exposing Marie's toned stomach. In one swift motion, the Wolf kneed Marie in her stomach with such force that blood expelled from her mouth. Marie dropped to her knees. The Wolf's power was astonishing – it was like she wasn't even trying. Then, in an unexpectedly gentle gesture, the Wolf placed her index finger beneath Marie's bloody chin.

I could see the Wolf whispering something in Marie's ear. Her eyes flickered with fear, and she abruptly reverted back to her normal Demon form. What did the Wolf say to her? Something was wrong, but at least she was still conscious. She rose to her feet. This was odd, Marie walking away from a challenge. There was just no way. I broke into a run.

"Marie!" I shouted as I met her halfway. "Are you okay, what's wrong, are you hurt?"

Marie began to tear up, trying her hardest not to cry. I pulled her close as she began to crack.

"Marie, what happened over there? Tell me, please," I whispered.

"She...knows, Tyler..." Marie sobbed.

"Knows what? Marie, talk to me!" She was crying hysterically now.

"She said you have to fight her! Or she's going after Logan and Harley, and then your parents!"

I looked past Marie's shoulder as I held her. I could see the Wolf waiting for me.

No way out of this one, but I'll be damned if I'm going to let this lady threaten my kids! I kissed Marie on the cheek reassuringly.

"I'm...I'm sorry, sweets, this time it's all you. Just don't die, okay?" Marie said, her voice faltering. Before I could walk away, Marie quickly grabbed my hand.

"There's something else, Tyler," she added.

Uh oh, something is definitely wrong. Marie never calls me by my name, it's usually sweets this, sweets that.

"I felt something weird when she grabbed me," said Marie, distraught. "It was like she was sucking the life out of me. I know Keith warned us about this, but I didn't want to believe I could be susceptible to it. Please, Tyler," she pleaded. "Be careful. Who knows what effect that power could have on you?"

I could tell by Marie's nervous tone that this was going to get ugly, and fast. I approached the Wolf until we were face to face. As we sized each other up, I couldn't help but notice she was pretty hot, in a Cate Blanchett kinda way.

What am I saying, now's not the time, Tyler! This lady wants to rip your face off.

"I'm glad you decided to join this little dance, Merozantine. I've witnessed your power, but now I wish to test my limits. And what a wise choice you made. I really hate killing children and the elderly."

I turned and looked back at Marie and the others. Marie's siblings all nodded their silent assent. Their faces grew dark with pain. Emily took Marie's hand. Preston put his huge arm around her shoulders. I had been living with this Demon blood for three weeks and felt like I had gotten a pretty good grip on it. Drawing Sardna from my tattered jeans pocket, I sized her up. The Wolf was tall for a woman, she had to be at least five-foot-ten. Her white hair and grey eyes pierced my soul. I wondered if it was some sort of mind game she was playing. I could feel her under my skin like some sort of annoying splinter. She eyed me up and down, head to toe, studying every twitch of my muscles.

"Who would have thought you'd be so handsome? Perhaps when I'm done beating you within an inch of your life, I'll kill your wife and keep you. Would you like that?" she teased.

"No thanks, I'm good. Let's just get this over with, I've got a shard to get home." I felt that confidence boost again, in spite of my nervously bubbling gut.

"Hum, very well," said the Wolf, clearly a little offended.

She wasted no time in throwing punches. I was shocked at how fast she was. Right, left, right, right – somehow, I was able to dodge the majority of them. The Wolf disappeared into purple smoke. I whipped my head around to try to get ahead of her next move. I found a punch to my stomach instead. She grabbed me out of mid-air by the neck, slamming me into the pavement like she was putting out the stub of a cigarette.

Now I'm mad.

I could feel the transformation beginning: my teeth were becoming sharp and my body was filling out and bulking up.

"There it is," the Wolf said with a toothy grin. "That's the power I want to see."

I picked myself up and clenched my blade; I knew it was time to kick things up a notch.

The Wolf lunged towards me. I managed to dodge as she punched a hole in a car behind me. As I rolled out of the way, I drew my blade, taking a swipe at the Wolf's side. It seemed as if I may have hit her before she vanished. But where did she go? I could feel she was close. Out of the blue the Wolf appeared in front of me, taking a swipe at my head with her long nails. I swiftly ducked, and thrusted the hit of my blade upward, bashing her in the chin.

That hit caused her to stagger. I had an opening, so I grabbed her by the fleece with my free hand and used my head for the only thing it's good for – I bashed her in the nose.

Now's my chance. I tried to go in for a final slice, but she recovered and blocked my slash with her sharp black fingernail, sliding it across my blade and kicking up sparks. *That's one heck of a manicure,* I thought. She was too quick. It was time for a new strategy.

Demon blood was not without its perks. Over the past three weeks, Nicole had taught me a few spells. Now that I was Demon, I was able to perform magic. Honestly, I didn't think much of those dusty books of hers at the time, but all the studying had paid off.

My favorites were Alacritous, a technique that gave me great speed, and Conflagration, which was a big flame spell. Combine the two and I was pretty much Super Mario with the fire flower after five energy drinks. I unloaded flame after flame on the Wolf. There was so much smoke and dust I couldn't see, but I knew I had her on the ropes. I began to let up on my attack, to clear the area of smoke. I whipped my head around, but couldn't lock her in my sights. Where could she be hiding?

Ouch! Out of the smoke she decked me, knocking me to the ground face first.

Wow, she put some serious muscle behind that one. My head was spinning, my ears were ringing, and I was now on the ground spitting out blood. She was using my own debris against me, treating it like camouflage.

My vision was doubled, but I could see her standing above me as I rolled over. Maybe she had knocked some sense into me. She was zapping my strength with every punch. *I have an idea,* I thought. *I'll back myself into a corner and use one of the frost bombs that Nicole gave me.* They didn't look like much, just little blue orbs -- pretty dainty, to be honest. I wasn't sure if I should throw it at the Wolf or into a warm bath. I checked in with my aching body -- the bath sounded pretty damn good right about then.

Scurrying across the floor like a frightened mouse, I tried to put enough distance between the Wolf and me. I had to time it just right. In the gradually dissipating smoke, I saw movement. Swiftly, the Wolf appeared through the smokescreen and jabbed her sharp claws towards my chest. I quickly dashed to a corner and reached in my pocket for the first bomb and hurled it at the Wolf.

It was a terrible throw – I completely missed. I think Harley has a better throwing arm than me.

With only one orb left, I had to make it count. I tossed it with everything I had. The Wolf jabbed again, puncturing the orb like a child's bath bubble and freezing her in her tracks. I, however, was unfazed because of the Conflagration spell. My body was still super-heated, and I could see the glowing hot energy emitting from my hands. The ice melted off of me like a freezy pop at high noon in summertime.

"It's about time you chilled out, Wolfie!" I proudly exclaimed. What a lame pun. But I'm like the Michael Jordan of dad jokes. *Swish,* I thought, chuckling to myself.

I had hardly turned away before I heard a cracking sound, like ice cubes in a warm glass of water. "You've got to be kidding me," I muttered.

The Wolf was vibrating, the ice cracking from all angles until it shattered like glass. The Wolf stood there in all of her arrogance, cracking her neck.

"You're a clever one, I'll give you that. Definitely a better tactician than fighter. But this ends here."

I was fresh out of ideas, locked in a one-on-one deathmatch with a rabid Lassie with fists. My stomach began to churn. It felt as if my insides would soon come out of my mouth. I was so weak from this fight that I had changed back to my human form. Once again, I was just an idiot holding a sad little toothbrush.

As I stood waiting for Wolf to deliver on her promise, Fortune smiled upon me. Lightning sliced a zigzag through the sky, followed by a thunderous crack. The reverberations were still ringing in my ears when some strange armored knight-looking guy appeared in front of me. I hoped and prayed that he was on our side, because I wasn't exactly in fighting form. I had to admit, though, I was jealous of his look. I suddenly felt kind of lame by comparison, in my hoodie and tattered skinny jeans. The knight was covered from head to toe in ash-black armor, his pauldrons as dark as the October sky. A large broadsword lay across his hip. His eyes were glowing through the slit in his visor. He turned to face the Wolf.

"And who might you be? No matter, this has nothing to do with you. I recommend you run along," the Wolf said dismissively to the Knight. I slowly began to back away. *Looks like I'm off the hook as far as this fight goes.* I glanced over at Marie and the others down the street. They were gesturing at me about something, but I couldn't tell what. The knight said nothing. Instead, his visor began to glow a hot red, and his armor started heating up like a metal skewer plunged into a flame.

Marie's voice popped into my head.

"Sweets, this guy looks serious, get out of there now!"

"Oh, hey Marie, listen, I really am sorry about the whole..."

"SHUT UP AND RUN, DUMMY!" shouted Nicole as she chimed in on our moment.

Point taken. As I started to sprint away, I glanced back at the knight, wondering who this guy was. And was the Wolf really arrogantly standing there like she was invincible? I felt like I had to say something. The metal man shot out a bright red beam, the force of which cracked the street pavement, rupturing fire hydrants along the way. The Wolf was clearly in the line of fire, but she wasn't budging.

"Are you insane! Move, stupid!" I shouted at the Wolf as concrete dust clogged the air. The magnitude of the blast was prodigious. It blew me off my feet on my way back to Marie and the others, forcing me to take shelter in a sliver between two buildings. The dust was burning my eyes and clogging my lungs. Visibility was terrible and I couldn't make heads from tails. As the air began to settle, I poked my head out from my refuge. I could see the knight. He still stood firmly, his legs slightly apart, arms at his sides, armored hands clenched into fists. If he was moving at all, I couldn't see it. Steam was rising from his armor the way it does off of pavement after a summer rain. And across from him, still standing where she had been just moments before, the Wolf. I had to rub my eyes again before my brain absorbed what my rods and cones were telling me. She had a giant hole through her torso.

"I... I can't...what...?" murmured the dying Wolf.

Her body fell to the pavement, eyes wide open. They stared into nothing like the eyes of a doll. As I cowered out of my narrow hiding place, the knight turned to me and gave a barely perceptible nod as he vanished into formlessness. For once in my life, I was speechless.

I ran to join Marie and the others. They looked every bit as perplexed as I was. Was this a victory? It felt anticlimactic, somehow.

Marie stepped over the rubble and threw her arms around me. "I'm so glad you're okay, sweets. You fought so well!" I shrugged, feeling like I didn't deserve the praise.

"I don't know, Marie. I don't think I would have won that if that weird knight hadn't shown up. The Wolf would have killed me. What the hell was that, anyway?"

"I have no idea," said Preston, swiping dust from his shirt and the front of his pants as he joined us. "But I have the feeling we'll find out sooner or later, whether we want to or not."

Emily nodded in agreement. "The enemies we're facing aren't the sort to throw in the towel. We can't let down our defenses." She had spoken out loud the edgy feeling we were all experiencing. It felt too quiet.

I guess I shouldn't have been complaining. We had retrieved the third shard with only one left to go. But there was a strangeness in the air. Both Marie and I were worried for our children and wondered who else knew about where they were – even though neither of us said it, I know we were both rolling all of the terrifying possibilities around in our minds. It didn't take Demon telepathy to understand that much.

Marie had been relieved to see me in one piece after Wolf's demise, but I knew she was still angry about the secret I had kept from her. She walked apart from me and Nicole and wouldn't look at Emily or Preston. None of us spoke as we left the battlefield. I knew some of us would be licking our wounds for days to come.

VIII
No Rest for the Wicked

I stared at the ceiling fan in the dark. It was three o'clock in the morning and my mind was racing, but its shell, my beaten-down body, was exhausted. These last few months had been brutal. I was so tired all the time – chronic fatigue was putting it lightly. It was a struggle just to have my head in the game, whether I was at the office or at home with the kids.

I groaned like an old man as I sat up in our mussed bed. *Maybe I should just watch some TV*, I thought. *Good old mindless television should do me some good.* Maybe there was a Fresh Prince of Bel Air rerun playing.

I felt my skin prickling from the heat. It was the kind of dry heat that filled your mouth with cotton. I looked to the dresser for my glass of water and noticed that Marie wasn't in bed with me. I had been so lost in thought that I hadn't even realized I was alone.

I put myself in her shoes: so close to seeing her dad awake and in one piece; so close to going home after who knows how many years away. I'd probably be sleepless, too, knowing how much was at stake. Hell, I *was* sleepless, roaming the hallways of our home at all hours of the night.

This castle we lived in was strange, to say the least, but tonight it seemed even more so. I could hear every creak, feel every bump in the night. I was so on edge, the back of my neck felt like it had a thousand pins in it.

That's a strange glowing red light in the kitchen. Maybe Marie is working on a spell or something.

"Marie, whatcha doing?" I called as I hit the kitchen corner. "Hey, what the heck is this?... Is this...blood?" I whispered as I touched the stone wall.

I turned the corner into the kitchen and everything in me went cold.

It was Marie. She was sprawled on the floor and there was blood everywhere. I dashed over to her and sat her up on my lap.

"Oh god, oh god, oh god, oh god, oh god. Please, be okay, please," I whispered in desperation, brushing her dark hair away from her face. It was heartbreaking to see her so vulnerable. I would never admit this to her out loud, but Marie was the rock in our family unit – it often seemed like nothing could scare her.

I could barely keep a grip on her body, the blood was so slippery. I looked around me, momentarily lost for what to do next. Seeing Marie's phone on the edge of the counter, I reached for it. Juggling the phone and Marie in my bloody hands, I dialed for an ambulance. The receiver was silent. The call wouldn't connect. I looked at the screen.

"What! No service? Zero bars? You've got to be kidding me!"

Tossing the phone to the side, I searched all over Marie, trying to find the wound. If I could just apply pressure... There was blood everywhere, was I too late? I gently placed her back on the wet floor and dashed upstairs to get my phone. It, too, had no bars. I tried to dial anyway, becoming more enraged with each failed call.

"Hold on Marie, just hold on!" I called as I ran to the front door. "Help! Someone, please!" I screamed, my voice cracking.

Astonishing, you would think someone would come running out

of their house upon hearing screaming in the middle of the night. I stood in my underwear staring out at the dark street. It was eerily silent. Not even crickets.

No one was coming.

I ran back into the house. But Marie's body was gone.

"What...what the heck is going on?" I said, panting.

A trail of blood was heading upstairs. She must have gotten up. I ran up the steps two at a time. All I could do was pray I'd find Marie healing at the top.

"Marie! Marie!!" I screamed.

In my panic at finding Marie, I had momentarily forgotten about the kids. My heart nearly stopped when I thought about what state I'd find them in, after seeing their mother covered in blood. I busted through the children's door and pulled back their blankets in a flash. They were gone. The sheets were cold. What the hell was going on here?

"No, no, please no," I moaned, slamming my fist against the floor.

That's when I heard a groan, followed by a loud yep and whimper. I jumped to my feet and dashed down the hall. The scene that met me was heartbreaking. Bronx was lying in the corner at the end of the hallway, a stiletto blade protruding out of his neck.

"Bronx, no, buddy, please, not you, too?" I sobbed.

As I collapsed onto the disheveled runner carpet by my dog, I felt a cold breeze trickle down my back. I turned to look over my shoulder. A man in a black trench coat was standing behind me. He was a younger Asian man, perhaps in his twenties, with hair the color of coal. He wore large silver gauntlets upon his hands and a menacing smile from ear to ear, as if he enjoyed what he had just done.

"YOU!" I growled, standing up. "You did this! You're one of the Madonna, aren't you? What did you do with Marie and my children?" I pelted him with questions, my rage building.

The figure continued to smile eerily.

"Well, aren't you going to say anything? I want answers!" I screamed.

"Don't you mean, what did you do? he hissed.

I looked down. I was holding Marie; she had appeared out of thin air. I dropped to my knees, cradling her in my arms.

I began to stroke her hair with my blood-stained hands, overcome with emotion. I had to save her somehow. She was whispering something. I craned my head to hear her.

"How...how...could you?" came her voice, quiet and hoarse.

"What?"

A dagger appeared in my left hand. What had I done?

I gently placed Marie down on the floor. I placed my fingers over her eyelids, gently closing them. I couldn't hold back my tears. I hurled the dagger at the mysterious figure, cracking him into a thousand pieces. Marie came through where the figure had been standing moments ago. She was completely naked and covered in blood, broken glass fragmenting under her feet with each step.

"Is this what you want, sweets? Do you like what you see?" she seductively whispered.

In a puff of purple smoke, Marie had changed into her Demon form and grabbed me by my throat. She was way too strong; fighting her off wasn't possible. She lifted me off the ground, choking me little by little. I couldn't breathe. It felt as if water were filling my lungs.

The edges of my vision were going black.

I sprang up in bed, screaming at the top of my lungs. Marie sat up, too, furious with me.

"What in the world is your problem, Tyler!" Marie shouted. "Please! Go to sleep. All you do anymore at night is fidget and fidget. I just worked three twelve-hour shifts in a row, man!"

She lightly smacked me with the back of her hand, sighed loudly, and beat her pillow into submission before shoving her face back into it. From inside the fabric and feathers, I heard a short, frustrated scream.

I hadn't yet come down from my nightmare. My heart was pounding wildly. The digital clock blared the time at me in neon yellow: three a.m.

Boy oh boy, did morning come quickly. The day started out like any other: I woke up, got the kids and myself ready, fed Bronx (I lingered over him a little longer that morning, petting his neck where the dagger had been). I even gave him a few extra treats before I hit the road.

Great, oodles of traffic on the way to school this morning, just my luck. To make my drive even more frustrating, my two little monsters decided to have a screaming match in the backseat. But hey, as long as no one was burning the upholstery with fire magic, I was good.

Finally, we made it to the school.

I pulled up to the crosswalk to let the kids out as usual. They walked into the building, pushing and shoving each other the entire way. I put the car in drive and began to inch forward to let a minivan pull in behind me. During the crawl, I let my eyes wander along the sidewalk. Kids were running to the building, parents handing off bookbags and lunch boxes, a teacher outside conversing with a colleague.

Then I saw him.

It was the guy from my dream: the black trench coat, silver gauntlets -- definitely him. He hadn't looked my way and was beginning to walk off of the school campus. I abruptly threw the car into park and jumped out.

"Hey, hey you!" I shouted, picking up my stride. A couple of car horns honked behind me. A mom yelled for me to move my car. I ran up to the guy and grabbed him by his sleeve. "Don't ignore me, I said stop!" The guy swung around and gave me a perplexed look. It wasn't him.

"Umm, sorry man, I thought you were someone else," I murmured apologetically.

Man, I had to get a grip. First, night terrors; now I was heckling guys on the street. I felt like I was losing my marbles. But that was definitely him that I saw, at least I was nearly sure. I mean, who wears gauntlets on a regular basis?

At work, my whole day was out of sync. I had hit a wall in my productivity. I was fixated on two things: the last piece of the sword, and the crazy nightmare I had. My head was pounding. It had been a week and nothing, not a single lead on the last sword piece.

"Hey, Tyler...Tyler! We're off to lunch, man, catch you in a bit," my coworker called.

"Yeah sure, no worries," I absently replied.

I was alone now in the office; just me and the humming of forty computers.

Usually the office was as cold as an igloo. However, today it was sweltering. I supposed it wasn't that strange; it was an older building, after all. Maybe the central air was on the fritz.

I at least thought, by now, I'd get a vibe on the shard. Speaking of vibes, what was that noise? It was a low gurgling sound like a giant empty stomach. It sounded as if it came from the restroom.

The restroom was above the office. I headed toward the source of the sound.

Wait, wait, hold on, Tyler, you've seen plenty of horror movies. Keep your eyes peeled for anything weird. God, with my luck it'll be a killer doll.

I looked around cautiously as I entered, and my eyes fixed on a sink. It was nothing monumental or scary after all, just the water running. "Why is it so hard for people to turn the water off," I griped to myself. As I turned around to reach for a paper towel, I wondered if my mind was beginning to play tricks on me after all. The water was back on. I reached for the faucet again, and the white fluorescent lights began to flicker. This was more than just bad wiring.

"Now what?" I mumbled.

This time the sink shut off on its own, and the pipes began to rumble and rattle. I stepped back in fear of a water geyser, but the shaking came to an abrupt halt. I slowly backed my way toward the exit, fumbling for the door handle with my eyes still trained on the sink.

The sink began to run again, spouting blood this time instead of water. The lights cut out, engulfing the bathroom in darkness, even though it was still midday outside. The mirrors fogged up and it began to feel like a rainforest from hell. I was petrified. My childhood self would have definitely peed his pants by now. Turning to the door, I shook the handle with all my strength. I tried to make a break for the cobweb-covered window, and that's when I heard a loud, long hiss.

"What the—hmmmmfff!"

I tried to get my words out, but gooey silk covered my mouth. Before I could come up with an escape strategy, my feet were bound together, and I was flipped upside-down. Eight prickly legs began to twist and turn my body, wrapping me up like a mummy, with only my head exposed. I felt the blood rushing into my skull. To my hor-

148

ror, a large brown spider hung in front of my face. My eyes grew as big as saucers and I could feel myself trembling.

"My, my, my, what a tasty treat this is," hissed the giant spider.

God, I hate spiders, and now I'm spider chow. What a way to go, Tyler!

"My master gave me permission to do whatever I want with you," it continued, stroking my face with a prickly foot. "But don't you worry. I promise I'll be gentle."

The creature pushed my head to one side, exposing my neck, and bit down with its fearsome hollow fangs. I felt the venom pumping into my veins. My eyes began to roll into the back of my skull.

"Ma…rie…" I mumbled as I slowly began to lose consciousness.

I came to on the bathroom floor, the water overflowing from the shallow porcelain sink. As I lay on the floor, the radiator began to hiss. Steam filled the bathroom.

Oh crap, could this be another dream?

Out of the steam stepped a figure. It was the man in the trench coat. Seeing him again, I was now convinced it had been him outside of my kids' school.

"So, you're the Merozantine," the man in the trench coat said. I sat on the cold wet floor, my fist clenched and blood pressure rising.

"Yeah, it's me! First, I got rid of the big guy, then the flaming dude, and finally, Wolf. Can you guess who's next?" I boldly shouted.

"Tell me, boy, where are the shards?" the man said, ignoring my threat. "It would be wise of you to surrender them to me."

"Over my dead body," I said. Such a cliché, but I had nothing else. I hadn't gotten any real sleep in what felt like forever. Even now I was having trouble just convincing myself to stand up.

The figure kneeled on the wet tile floor, leaning to whisper into my ear. I could feel his cold breath on my neck, and goosebumps began to ripple across my skin as he spoke. "That sounds exquisite," he whispered, licking his lips. "By the time I'm done you'll pray for death."

Does this crap ever end? I feel like these bad guys are constantly heckling me.

"You are free to go, Merozantine. Be a good lad and lead me to my quarry."

With those words, he vanished. It was clear now who I was dealing with. He was a Madonna, no doubt about it. Keith couldn't have been more on point about how dangerous this guy was. How was I supposed to deal with an enemy that haunted my dreams?

I thought, quite suddenly, of McKenzie. She didn't have great magic powers like her siblings. However, she did have the unrivaled ability to detect energy. Maybe I could have her act as a smoke detector. No -- a nightmare detector!

This was indeed a superb plan, and I wasted no time in patting myself on the back for it. There was just one wrinkle: McKenzie had the worst self-esteem; she was unlikely to agree to this. Very rarely did she appear in her Demon form or use magic. I had a hunch that she actually enjoyed being viewed as a human. I had to be very delicate in my execution.

"Pleeeeeaaaassse, McKenzie! Pretty please! You won't even have to lift a finger, just tell me when he's getting close. Then guide me telepathically while I'm inside his dreamworld!" I was a master of negotiation.

"No, absolutely not!" McKenzie firmly replied.

"Why not? This could seriously save my skin. We'll have one less Madonna to deal with, and we'll be one step closer to reviving your dad," I begged.

"What if I mess up? What if I accidentally get you killed? I think we should be focusing on finding the last piece of the sword. Not provoking a Madonna."

"Actually, that's part of my plan."

"And what *is* **this 'plan' of yours, Tyler?» McKenzie snapped.**

"Simple," I said, knowing that the last thing I could depend on was simplicity. "I'll get the last piece to the sword, which will draw him close. This is where you'll come in. Once I'm pulled into his dream world, you tell me where his energy level is so I can attack him. You'll pretty much have to be my eyes." This was a horrible plan, but I smiled at her reassuringly anyway.

"I don't know, Tyler, last time you didn't tell Marie your plan and look at what happened." She looked concerned. "Is she still mad at you?"

"She is, but I really can't involve her. Not this time. The last thing I want is for this guy to toy with her mind while she's taking care of patients. Marie loves her job. One bad medical error could ruin her career." It seemed I finally had McKenzie convinced.

She sighed deeply. "Okay, but just this once, and then no more favors!"

"Yesss!" I exclaimed. "I owe you big-time."

The next day, McKenzie and I met up with Preston. The last piece of the sword had proven to be extremely difficult to locate. We had nearly given up. Preston had already scanned pretty much the entire planet.

"I'm out of ideas, bro," said Preston. "There's nothing on the planet that even remotely gives off a signal similar to interstellar energy. I'm tapped. What about you?"

"Pssshh, don't look at me," I responded. "I'm still trying to figure out the whole Demon thing."

"Guys, this might be a long shot, but…what if we can't find the shard on Terra, because it's inside of Terra, somehow?" said McKenzie.

"Holy crap, she might be right!" I cried. "What if the shard is deep in the planet itself, like a fossil?"

Preston began to twist and turn his Windfall Stone, projecting all sorts of algorithms. Angelic and demonic hieroglyphs floated across the air.

"Well, you were half-right, sis," said Preston, examining the projections. "And you were half-right, too, Tyler."

"What? Really?" I shouted.

Preston pointed to a spot on the map. The Museum of Natural History in New York City.

Unbelievable. All this time, the shard had been stuck in the bone of an old bear. Preston surmised that the magical properties of the shard must have fused it to the bone structure of the animal while it was alive, which was highly possible, given that Daevas' kids had arrived on Terra around the fifteenth century along with the pieces of the sword. The timing definitely lined up.

"Hey, take a look at this." Preston zoomed in with a twist and a turn on his Windfall Stone. He focused onto a plaque attached to the bear exhibit:

The Goliath Bear

The last sighting of this species was recorded in 1502. This particular bear roamed the village of Glenhyde, Scotland, and was known to be a maneater. Stories passed down through history tell of a legend in which this bear was responsible for the death of the heroic knight, Sir Everard Ashdown, in 1470. After the bear killed and ate a family on the outskirts of the village, Ashdown swore to avenge the gruesome act and pursued the bear on foot, armed only with his sword. The villagers found Ashdown's body in Dewitt Forest the following day, by all appearances mauled by a bear. His sword was broken in half, and only the lower half, containing the hilt, was found in the vicinity.

In fact, evidence discovered during recent restoration efforts points to sword-wounds on several areas of the skeleton. This only fueled the fire of the legend, encouraging it to live on in the collective imagination.

The story was unbelievable. However, nothing shocked me anymore. Angels, Demons, fairies, goblins – at this point, I would have wholeheartedly believed in the Easter Bunny.

"I suppose you're going to tell me this isn't a legend at all, and that it all really happened," I said.

"I would assume that's the case," said McKenzie.

"So, Tyler," said Preston, "How much do you want to bet that our friend Mr. Ashdown's sword was fused with our shard? I'm also willing to bet that his sword broke off into our friend the bear here."

"Thus, fusing with the bear over time, prolonging his power and life, no doubt," McKenzie added. "If he was a maneater before, I'd hate to imagine what he was like after he won that fight."

"Exactly!" said Preston.

"That's crazy!" I shouted. "My question is, how is it we found the first shard in a tree, but couldn't detect this piece stuck in some old bone?"

"Well, the logical answer would be because of the size difference between shards. This shard is much smaller; therefore, it emits a lower energy frequency," said Preston as he compared shards via the Windfall Stone. "It could also be that fusing with an intact sword and then being absorbed into a living bone which eventually became fossilized further disguised the broken piece. I'm just glad we seemed to have sniffed it out before our enemies did. I guess even the archaeologists didn't think to X-ray this particular bone."

Well, I guess it was off to New York. However, we couldn't simply waltz into a world-renowned museum and say, "I'll have the famous bear fossil, please." We were going to have to sneak in. Luckily for me, my family consisted of Demons who could use magic. Piece of cake.

Later that night, Preston, McKenzie, and I met in secrecy. We used those horrible Wanderlust Lockets to transport us directly inside the museum. Now that I had my dinner in reverse, it was time to get to work.

God, this place is huge, I thought, looking around. *Where are we supposed to start?*

It appeared as if we were somewhere on the bottom level. Six grand marble pillars rose to the ceiling, cradling a stunning glass window. It was a beautiful night, and the light from the full moon ticked across a stegosaurus' spine like an Egyptian sundial.

We wanted to be careful not to jeopardize the plan, so splitting up was not an option.

"Man, I can't see anything in here!" I whispered loudly.

"The lights aren't on," Mckenzie whispered back, stating the obvious.

"You'd think they would have emergency backup lights or something," chimed Preston.

"Yeah, 'cause nothing says jail time like breaking into a museum and turning on the lights!" I sarcastically hissed.

I was slowly beginning to question who I had recruited for this mission. I was now more worried that Shaggy and Scooby here would do something dumb.

"I got us covered," replied Preston. He reached out his large hand and created a ball of light, just big enough to cover his palm. We all congregated around the information desk, just below the skull of a triceratops -- my second favorite dinosaur, in case you were wondering. We began scouring the countertops and pamphlets for answers.

"Hang on, why didn't we look this information up online before we left?" I whispered.

I was beginning to see why Marie or Nicole always ran point.

"Here! Third floor," McKenzie excitedly whispered. "It's the 15th-century exhibit, flown in from Europe."

The three of us hastily ran through the high-ceilinged rooms as the moonlight shimmered and intermittently cast ghostly spotlights on us. Soon, we were face-to-face with destiny. The last piece, our holy grail. I placed my hand on the bear skeleton's shoulder. I could feel the shard; this was really it. My head became light and woozy. But something else was here, something besides the shard.

"McKenzie," I gulped. "Get ready, he's here."

I looked around me. I was back on the first floor of the museum. It appeared to be a European exhibit on Knights and Dragons. I knew something was off. We had entered on the first floor, and I saw no such thing – and on top of it, Preston and McKenzie were both gone. An eerie fog rolled across the floor. My breath fogged in front of my face, each inhale stinging my chest as goosebumps danced across my skin. I closed my eyes and began to concentrate; I could hear McKenzie clear as a bell. I just hoped this would work or I was a dead man.

"Okay, McKenzie you're up, can you see anything?" I asked, tapping my earlobe as if it were a headset.

"Yup, I can see and hear everything you can," replied McKenzie.

"Hold on ... 'see'?" Did this mean Marie could see what I saw

when she was in my head? I shuddered at the thought. Talk about invasion of privacy.

"Hey McKenzie, just out of curiosity, can Marie 'see' through my eyes as well?"

"Well, yeah," McKenzie replied. *"That's like Telepathy 101."*

Walking through the empty museum hall, I could hear a faint ticking sound echoing off of the arched ceiling. At first it reminded me of a wind-up toy. But every step I took was mirrored by a clank. I could hear the metal clunking and creaking, churning and squeaking, growing closer by the second.

As the sound inched closer, a suit of armor appeared out of the shadows. It was a well-polished silver suit, robotic in its movements. I drew Sardna as the armor drew its blade. I looked to my left and right. Other pieces of armor began to surround me. I ran toward the armor, ready to strike. I felt a warm tingle moving through my head, like someone peeing in my skull – hopefully minus the smell: McKenzie's voice.

"Tyler, stop!" McKenzie shouted. I came to a screeching halt, sliding through the fog wafting across the shiny museum floor. I nearly crashed into a velociraptor posed within lush jungle scenery.

"He's above you!"

I sheathed my blade and swung it upwards with all my strength. A loud crash echoed through the museum. The man in the trench coat had toppled to the ground, sliding across the floor and smashing into a mammoth leg, tipping a pile of bones onto his head. Seizing upon the chance, I charged towards him as he emerged from the prehistoric rubble, brushing dust from his coat. He held a gauntlet up in front of his face, stopping me cold in my tracks. I was frozen – he was using telekinesis to lift my body from the ground.

"That was, as you pests on Terra say, 'a free one.' It won't happen again," he said.

I had forgotten that demons specialized in telekinesis. He rose to his feet and began walking toward me. He was disheveled from his fall, and I could hear his loose metal coat buckle smacking the floor in tempo with his steps.

"Allow me to formally introduce myself. I am called Catacomb. I am one of the Beast of the Madonna."

He raised his other hand, turning it so that his palm was up. My body followed suit, flipping upside down. He began to swing me back and forth like a pendulum.

"This is my realm. I make the rules here. I decide who lives and who dies!"

I tried to draw my sword, but my body was in a state of suspended animation. Growing up, I had seen all nine Nightmare on Elm Street movies through my fingers. As much as I hated to be scared, my mom was a big horror fan. Freddy Kruger, Aliens, Chucky, you name it. Heck, I still couldn't look at doll without thinking that it was out to get me. I knew how this worked. He was absolutely right; this was his realm, and even with McKenzie in my head, helping me, I couldn't win this fight. But if I could find a way to bring him back to reality, I might have a shot.

Catacomb used his powers to fling me across the hall like a used sock, slamming my face against a glass vitrine. I was now face-to-face with the crotch of an ice man. *Thank God for this thick layer of glass between us.* To my surprise and horror, the ice man began to move, bashing his club against the thick glass. I had to get out of this twisted universe!

If I could get close to him, maybe, just maybe, I could pull him back with me to the waking realm.

I began to concentrate as best as I could and reached out to McKenzie. *"McKenzie, can you hear me? I have an idea."*

"Go ahead Tyler, it's fuzzy but I hear you," McKenzie whispered in my head.

"Okay, it's going to sound crazy, but I need you to get my body as close to an alarm as possible. Doesn't matter what – a motion sensor, a roped-off exhibit. Then, trigger it!"

"What? No way, Tyler, are you insane? If I do that, the police will be here in no time. We wouldn't have time to get the shard."

"Just do it!" I demanded.

Suddenly, I heard Preston's voice.

"Just get close to him, bro, and hold on tight," he grumbled.

"Wait! Preston, you can get inside my head, too? Why hasn't anyone told me that this is a common ability?"

Wondering what he meant by "hold on tight," I stood up and charged at Catacomb. He moved his hand effortlessly, like he was batting away a fly. My body slammed back into the ground, sliding me in his direction. This was my chance. I grabbed the Madonna's leg as I slid past, holding on for dear life.

I was back in the real world almost immediately, the high-pitched squeal and red lights of the museum alarm blaring in my ears. Preston had picked up my sleeping body and hurled it into a glass case of Medieval jewelry, shocking me back to the land of the living. I would have appreciated a much lighter throw. My ankle was now entangled in the chain of a medallion. I frantically shook my legs, like a cat wearing shoes. I'd never really been a jewelry guy, and this was affirming my choices.

Moreover, upon returning to the land of the living, I wasn't alone. Lying next to me, covered in glass, was Catacomb. I had woken up next to a few strangers in my day, but this one hadn't even bought me a drink. Not to mention, he wasn't really my type.

Catacomb came to, and the two of us sprang to our feet. Now I was able to transform into Demon mode.

We wasted no time duking it out. Punch after punch, kick after kick, it felt like here in the real world we were evenly matched. And leaving the dream world was starting to take its toll on Catacomb. I punched him vigorously in his stomach, knocking him into the air. Catacomb tried his best to fight back, but he was far too drained. As his body hit the hard marble floor, the Madonna drew two blades from the silver holsters strapped to his thighs, making one last attempt to injure me. He charged toward me at lightning speed, cutting through the air like a ballistic missile. I evaded his knives, sliding underneath his thrust, jabbing Sardna through his torso. The Madonna stood over me, blankly looking into my eyes.

"As I said, you're next," I whispered to the Madonna.

For once, he didn't have a comeback. His dead eyes stared blankly as his body began to crystallize and slowly turn to smoke.

The alarm in the museum had gone silent, a sure sign that someone from the museum staff had arrived to follow up. The police would surely be next. Time was running out. Preston, McKenzie, and I returned to the bear fossil. I touched the bone that housed the shard. It grew warm under my palm, and I began to sweat and feel dizzy. The bone slowly cracked open, revealing our bounty.

"Grab it and let's get out of here!" McKenzie whispered, pulling out the Wanderlust Locket. I took a few uneven steps toward her. Preston grabbed my arm to prop me up, and we went out like a blink.

We had done it, and it was finally time to make things right.

Preston, McKenzie and I transported to the front lawn of the house. It was sometime after midnight. A warm summer rain was falling, the drops thrown into silhouette by the yellow porchlight.

Marie, Nicole, and Emily had caught on to what was happening and were standing in the doorway, waiting for us. I was prepared for the ear-beating of a lifetime but instead was greeted with warm embraces from Emily and Nicole, who spilled out the door to greet us.

"Well?" said Marie, taking a deep breath – probably to keep herself from yelling at me, I thought. "Did your little stunt pay off?" Her eyes began to bubble with tears. She threw her arms around me and squeezed me tightly, kissing my face, then abruptly broke away and ran to Preston and McKenzie. The five siblings huddled together, hugging and crying. I couldn't possibly fathom the joy they must have been feeling. I stood back and allowed them to have their moment.

"Hey, who's up for a cold one!" shouted Preston. "I think this calls for a celebration."

"Yeah Ty's, got any booze?" asked Emily. "I can't believe you pulled that off."

I looked over at McKenzie. She still seemed a little down. I felt like I should say something.

"Actually, it was all McKenzie. Even handed that Madonna his ass." I said with a smile. The others were in pure shock.

"Wow, look at you, little sis. Maybe you got a mean streak after all," said Nicole with a grin.

"Yeah," said Marie, "We knew you had something in ya!"

Preston made eye contact with me and gave a little nod of approval. I smiled back.

McKenzie's face lit up. It seemed like for the first time she felt like she was one of them.

I, on the other hand, had enough of feeling like a drowned rat. I went inside and lit the fireplace to warm our waterlogged bodies up from the rain. We all gathered around as if it was Christmas morning. We listened to some tunes, played a few drinking games, and ordered a bite to eat. I even woke up the kids and let them be a part of it. It felt so normal, the normal I had craved for far too long.

"So, what now, guys? What's the next step?" I asked, sipping my cold beer. The frosty glass felt good on my hot palm.

"I'm not actually sure," Marie replied. "Maybe put all the pieces together and see what happens?" We looked over at Preston, who simply shrugged.

Ugh, there was never a manual for these kinds of things. We gathered together all of the pieces, placing them gently on the shag carpet. We simultaneously held our breaths, waiting for...for what, exactly, none of us knew. Nothing was happening, no lightning bolts, no magic. We collectively exhaled with disappointment. For the first time ever, Marie and the others were just as confused as I was.

"What the hell!" yelled Nicole. "Do we have to solder this thing together or something?"

I looked at the pieces, scanning over each one carefully, bit by bit. I picked a shard up to further examine it. As I grabbed the shard, I accidentally pricked my finger.

"Ouch!" I winced, pulling my hand back as though something bit me. A couple of drops of blood fell onto the broken sword. "I hadn't expected something that old to be so sharp," I said, sucking the wound on my finger.

"Wait a tick, what's happening?" Emily said suddenly. We all looked down at the carpet.

The pieces began to shake and glow. The blade was repairing itself.

"Of course!" shouted Marie. "The sword responds to your blood! You're the last Merozantine!"

Right before our very eyes, Grus was becoming whole. Lightning surrounded the blade – it sparked and then the light was absorbed back into the sword. Immediately, it started to glow a bright purple. The magnitude of its power forced us all to stand back and marvel. The house shook. Wind was whipping around us, throwing pictures and objects all over the place. A great beam shot into the air, blasting a massive hole through the roof of our castle. Marie, Nicole, and Emily took to flight, following the beam.

"By the Old Gods' light!" shouted Nicole, "I think it's heading toward Dad! Could it really be…?"

"There's no thinking about it, sis. That's definitely where it's heading," Marie shouted back.

Preston, Mckenzie, and I were still grounded, transfixed by the pulsating blade. I tentatively reached my hand out, unsure of what could happen next. As I inched my hand closer, the sword stood upright, floating in mid-air. It paused for only a moment, and then began to dash around the room like a circular saw. Eventually the blade came to a screeching halt, the hilt landing in the palm of my hand.

This power is insane, I've never felt anything like this before! My head was ringing, and I felt feverish. It was as if it was too much power all at once. I was overdosing on energy. I could see and feel it all: The Merozantines, one after another; Camio, Loath; the Angels, the Demons; Transient humans; The Old Gods. My brain had been a dimly flickering bulb, now made bright. Yet it didn't stop there: I could hear Camio, and his plans, his thoughts. He wanted to use the Transients again, the humans here on Terra. He wanted to use our souls to power a weapon known as the Durendal Cannon.

"The souls of humanity will be the tide of destruction that brings forth the age of Demons. No Angels to build for, no Grootslang to combat, no Old Gods to rule us. The most powerful weapon in the cosmos engineered to be fueled by the souls of men."

My hands became clammy. I felt as if I was going to throw up.

"Tyler. Are you okay?" came Preston's voice beside me. He placed his large hand upon my shoulder. I was frozen like a deer in headlights, and Camio was driving the truck that would take out me and the rest of humanity.

"No" I replied. "I don't think I am. I saw Camio's vision! He's going to harvest the souls here on earth to power the Durendal Cannon. He's going to destroy half of the Empyrean Realm!"

"What? What do you mean?" Asked McKenzie.

"He's going to wipe out Dada, the Province of the Angels." Preston replied. "It appears our mission is far from over."

IX
Of Demons and Men

Marie and Nicole had been gone for a while now, and the sunrise would be appearing over the horizon in a matter of hours. I couldn't help but think the worst: maybe they were in trouble. What if they had run into a Madonna? One way or another I would have my answer soon. Emily had gone out solo to find them while Preston, McKenzie, and I stayed back with the kids, who had fallen asleep playing video games.

The smart thing would have been to try to get some sleep, but we were all too full of adrenaline to consider it. McKenzie was curled up on her side on the shag carpet, idly watching late-night television. She seemed to be staring past the screen, lost in her own thoughts. Preston was in the recliner, scrolling through his phone. I sat on the couch thoroughly examining Grus. What a blade! It was a long silver katana with black trim along the edges. The handle was shiny and inlaid with gold. It felt light, as though it was made of bird bones. I raised it in front of me and sliced it through the air a couple of times.

"Quite the impressive blade, huh Ty," said Preston.

"Yeah, it is! It makes my Sardna seem like a toy. Speaking of Sardna, what do I do with it now?"

"Well, I guess it would be wise to hold on to it. Who knows? Someday you might learn to dual wield," he said.

A series of loud thuds came from the part of the roof that hadn't been torn open. It was Marie, Nicole, and Emily. The sisters jumped through the gaping hole caused by Grus' self-repair – I tried to ignore the irony that fixing one thing had led to another thing breaking – and landed gracefully in tandem. Preston, McKenzie, and I jumped to our feet.

"You're back!" I said, overjoyed to see Marie and her sisters in one piece.

"Any luck? Did you find out where that beam went?" inquired Preston.

"Yeah," said Marie. "No doubt about it, that beam was for dad. We stopped by the hospital."

We held our breaths and leaned in with anticipation.

"And?!" the three of us shouted after several long seconds of silence.

Marie, Nicole, and Emily exchanged looks. It seemed as if they were deciding which one of them would break the news. After a pause, while the other two stared pointedly at her, Nicole cursed under her breath.

"Well…he's gone," mumbled Nicole.

"Define 'gone,'" asked McKenzie.

"Exactly what it sounds like, genius," snapped Nicole.

Gone! That was a good thing, right? So, what were we supposed to do now, put out a BOLO for this guy? If this worked and repairing Grus had snapped Daevas out of his coma, I assumed he had his powers back as well. Based on the tales I'd heard he was supposed to be crazy strong. What if he wasn't the same guy we once knew? What if he had memory loss and attacked us?

As I was wondering at all the variables, the roof above us began to shake thunderously, dust snowing down on us. *Oh great*, I thought, *the roof repair isn't expensive enough yet, let's tear off the rest of it.*

We could hear thumps and the clicking of metal dragging. Abruptly, the thumps stopped.

"What the heck is that?" asked Emily. We all braced ourselves for a fight.

Looking up through the hole in my roof, we caught a glimpse of a massive figure covered in shiny white armor. It seemed to focus its gaze down on us, and just as quickly as it had appeared, it stepped away and we could only see the stars in the night sky. The siblings and I glanced at each other, perplexed. Before any of us could ask a question, the figure had burst through the roof, creating a brand-new hole. As Emily and Preston took up the front line, readying for a fight, I ducked behind a couch.

"Why didn't he just use the hole that was there?!" I cried, exasperated as plaster and wood continued to rain down on us. As the dust settled and I peered over the side of the couch, I could see glowing blue eyes, visible through the giant's helmet.

The giant knight was eye-level with Preston, swinging his broad sword at him. Preston launched his morning star, wrapping it around the massive sword. The knight used this to his advantage and pulled Preston to the ground, morning star and all, as though he was a wooden marionette. The floor shook as he crashed into it, shoulder first. The knight raised his massive fist and punched Preston as he lay on the ground.

"Nicole, cover Preston!" I shouted.

Nicole tried lightning magic, conjuring a ball of bolts and hurling it at the invader. The knight deflected the blast, knocking Nicole aside. Now he was trotting in my direction. Each time his massive feet hit the floor, framed pictures rattled off of the walls, glass breaking on impact.

"Do you know how long it took me to hang all of those?" shouted

Marie as she flew at the knight. She kicked him square in his thick neck.

"What the heck, did he even feel that?" I mumbled.

The knight grabbed Marie's leg, swinging her around like a tornado. He launched her into a bookshelf, splintering the cedar. I drew Grus in midair, slashing downward on the mystery knight. He effortlessly blocked my attack. We began to duel in a whirlwind. Our blades crossed over and over again, predicting each other's moves as if each of our shadows belonged to the other.

"Wow, look at them go," I heard Preston say.

"I know," called Emily over the clashing of our swords. "Those two are putting on quite a show."

The knight's pace slowed, and he unwittingly began to let his guard down. I was out of breath, panting like Bronx after a good walk. I wasn't sure how much longer I could keep this up. Then, much to my surprise, the knight stepped back and lowered his sword. He slid it effortlessly back into its sheath and let out a great chuckle. Upon hearing this, Marie and the others began to laugh along. I was very confused; did I miss something?

"Wow, sweets," said Marie, chuckling, "You really have gotten powerful!" She crossed the room and hugged the massive knight.

The knight squeezed her around the waist with one arm, then let go and reached for his helmet. As he removed his visor, out popped out a blondish gray mustache, and squinty blue eyes the color of marbles. He removed the rest of his helmet, revealing a pair of large horns protruding through disheveled dirty-blonde hair.

"What's wrong, kid? Are you laying an egg, or crapping yourself?" He let out a great belly laugh. "Boy, you've gotten strong!"

I couldn't believe my eyes, but there he was: Marie's father. He was in Demon form, but it was the Dave I had always known. All our efforts had actually paid off. He was finally free. Preston stood up to shake his father's hand, his eyes welling up. Marie and the others surrounded Daevas and embraced him warmly, one after another.

It was truly a sweet and precious moment, with just one little issue. Why the hell did they destroy my house? I mean, first the hole in the roof became a chasm. Then they decided to turn my living room into an episode of Saturday Night Wrestling. I don't think I'll ever understand Demons. I mean, a nice sheet cake with "Welcome Home, Dad" written in frosting would have worked just fine!

"Alright, alright, that's enough of this horse crap!" shouted Daevas, in mock-gruffness. "How's about we crack open a cold one and get me up to speed?"

"We have a lot to talk about, sir," squawked Keith as he swooped in through my new homemade skylight. I thought I saw a bird in the corner of my eye during my little skirmish with Daevas. The real question is, why didn't the jerk give me some battle tips or at least offer a heads up?

"What the holy heck," grumbled Daevas, "Since when do birds talk in this realm?"

"Sir, it is I, Keith."

"Keith, how did you get like this?" asked Daevas.

"Dad, I think you should sit down first," chimed in Emily, cracking open a bottle and handing it to him. "We have a lot to catch you up on."

Two hours and three six-packs later, we had explained everything to Daevas about the Madonna, the shards, Keith's bird form, and my vision.

"So, Tyler," grunted Daevas. "Go over the vision part one more time."

I leaned back in my chair, took a deep breath and began to explain.

"Camio's plan was to give the Transients free will, by giving them souls and a realm in which they could populate: Terra. Once it was well-populated, he would invade Terra to use the souls of men to power the Durendal Cannon. He decided this would be an easier alternative than trying to subdue Grootslang. Somehow, he figured out that twenty human souls are equal to just one Grootslang soul, and in his mind, human souls are in abundance. Once the cannon is powered with the human souls, he plans on using it to wipe out Dada, the Province of Angels; and some group he called the Old Gods. Camio plans on repopulating Terra and Empyrean solely with Demons, making them the most powerful beings in existence, and enslaving the remaining Humans."

"I've always had my suspicions regarding Camio's loyalty to the kingdom. How has Loath not caught on yet? Too blinded by his own greed, I'm sure," mused Daevas.

I took a big gulp. I still couldn't believe we had made it this far. I had so much that I wanted to ask and say. But I couldn't seem to get the words out.

"What's wrong, son? You seem troubled," asked Daevas.

"Who, me?" I replied like a goof.

"No, the talking bird. Of course, you."

I opened my mouth, but nothing was spilling out – the epitome of the cat having my tongue.

"Look, I can't promise your safety through all of this," the old man grumbled. "But I can promise you this. While you and Marie are gone, those grandchildren will be under watchful eyes, as will your parents."

"I appreciate that Daevas, but if we're all going, who will stay?"

Daevas stretched out his arm, as Keith flew in and perched on it.

"Keith, you want to atone for your mistake, right?" asked Daevas in a low tone.

Keith tilted his head. "More than anything sir," squawked the bird.

"Well, this is your chance. I'm transferring you a little of my power. In the event that harm should find these kids, it's your duty to protect them at any cost. Is that clear?"

Even though Keith was a bird, his face said it all. He was overjoyed to have such a duty, and I couldn't express how grateful I was. Daevas stretched out his arm, releasing Keith to the wind.

"Go, fly to the Pine's residence and wait for Logan and Harley. We're counting on you."

And just like that, Keith was gone. I knew he wouldn't let us down.

Daevas sat back in the dining room chair, stroking his bushy mustache. The six of us were scattered about the living room. Together, we pondered our next move.

"So, when do we go back, dad?" Emily asked. "Is that even possible? Do you have the power to open a portal?" The room grew quiet; it was as if even our inner thoughts were holding their breaths.

"Watch your mouth! Don't ever question my abilities, am I clear!" shouted Daevas.

"Yes sir," she mumbled.

Daevas cracked open another cold beer, the foam building up in his mustache. He chugged the ale in a single breath.

"You kids need to listen! We can't go marching into Empyrean making threats without evidence. We need a strong case against Camio and Loath, as well as a solid plan of attack. If we go back, we need all of our ducks in line!"

"Well, where exactly do we get evidence from? Camio covered his tracks well, and the Synod believes anything out of Loath's mouth. It's a total wash," argued Marie.

"Like hell, it is," grunted Daevas. "I never trusted Loath or that snake, Camio. I knew deep down that they didn't have any interest in the greater good. I took the liberty of hiring a group of spies to keep track of both of them. A reliable pack of Demons who are only interested in the bottom line. They call themselves the Black Cicada Clan."

"The Black Cicada Clan?" asked Nicole, as the rest of us tilted our heads. I laughed inwardly; it made me think of Bronx tilting his head, curiosity peaked, whenever he heard the words "walk" or "treat" in conversation.

"Who the heck are they? How come I've never heard of these dudes?" Marie inquired.

"'Cause you don't know everything, that's why," grumbled Daevas. He took a sip of his beer before explaining, "When the universe was in its infancy, the Old Gods governed and made decisions on Empyrean. Eventually they got tired of dictating the lives of Demons and Angels. They made a decision to put someone on the throne. Many fought for this honor, but only one was chosen. After some discussion, the Old Gods held a series of games to determine the winner. They were called The Trials of Dunamis. The winner of the games would claim the title of King. After a grueling twelve days, an Angel by the name of Araqiel I was the victor. He won the games and became Empyrean's new ruler."

"Wait a second." Nicole interjected. "Araqiel I? I thought all this time Araqiel was the original king of Empyrean."

"Right!" Marie chimed in. "How come we've never heard of this tale, dad?"

"Well, if ya'd give me a minute I'll get there!" Daevas shouted. It felt just like old times, before Daevas fell ill and I got more than I had bargained for when I learned the truth about my wife and her

172

family. But no matter how many horns and batwings you throw in the mix, some things never changed: Marie and her siblings going nuts, and Dave – or rather, Daevas – telling them to "knock off the horse shit." It definitely felt familiar. I smiled and shook my head.

"Araqiel would go on to be an amazing ruler," Daevas continued. "He unified Angels and Demons in a time when the two could not and would not see eye to eye. There were all kinds of attempts on the young King's life, which is why he organized the The Black Cicada Clan. A group of six soldiers whose sworn duty was to not only protect the King, but to provide preventative maintenance to any potential threats."

"What happened to these Black Cicadas, dad?" asked Preston.

Daevas stroked his bushy mustache and looked up at the ceiling, as if he were gathering his thoughts.

He continued, "One day the king became ill. Mages and oracles tried everything to save him. But he was too far gone. Many rumors circulated that the King was poisoned by Demon assassins. If that was true, it would unravel everything he fought for. The flames of these rumors were quickly extinguished, and his son, Araqiel II, inherited the crown. But the thing is, Araqiel II wasn't exactly fond of his father. Behind closed doors he had suffered a rough childhood."

Daevas took a sip of his beer, and his brow furrowed. I read it as sympathy. He could put his kids in their place without a second thought, but I knew he was a warm and loving guy, who never raised his hand to them.

"As for the Black Cicada Clan, their oath is to serve only one master. Araqiel's death led them to take work as mercenaries. But one of the young Cicada befriended Araqiel as a kid. That Cicada would go on to form his own unit, whose duty would be to protect the new king. He agreed to remain behind as his bodyguard. The young soldier called on the Black Cicadas whenever he needed backup."

It didn't take long to put two and two together. Marie's father was that bodyguard. He must have formed the Knights of the Sistine Madonna to protect Araqiel II just as the Black Cicadas had protected Araqiel I.

"What's your move then, dad?" Preston cautiously asked.

"My move? Son, I have the game rigged," scoffed Daevas. "I've always been suspicious of Loath. The Black Cicadas have been following him closely since the day he was removed from the Synod. And they didn't disappoint. The Cicadas couldn't intervene but managed to record Loath's attack on the Demon village on a Windfall Stone. That same night the Madonna and I brought him to justice, Araqiel swore these events to secrecy. Araqiel is a good man, but often burdened by the dilemma of politics. He had no knowledge of the Cicada's involvement or the intel they got. I knew he wouldn't run the risk of triggering a civil war within the kingdom."

Daevas cleared his throat, lost in thought. He reached into a pouch attached to his waist and removed a wooden pipe and a package of loose tobacco. Stuffing it to the brim, he lit it and inhaled contemplatively, then smoothly exhaled. A large cloud of smoke hovered over the table. I stifled a cough, surprised that Marie hadn't freaked out over smoking in her house.

"If word ever got out about this footage it would immediately be destroyed. So, I hid it in plain sight." Daevas slid his chair back, rose to his feet and polished off his beer. I could tell from the expressions on the others' faces that they wanted to know where it was hidden as much as I did. Daevas faced Marie and motioned for her to stand. She raised a skeptical eyebrow, but the look on his face told her not to argue. Placing one hand on her shoulder, Daevas reached for the large purple jewel around her neck. He lifted the stone into the air, examining it under the tungsten living room lights.

"Hidden in plain sight," whispered Marie.

Daevas activated the jewel. The room lit up, projecting a bright red holograph of grainy footage. It was the night Loath slaughtered the Demon village. I glanced at Marie. I could tell she was furious, seeing something so gruesome happening to innocent people, especially the children. And there I was, upset at the poor film quality despite it coming from such an advanced civilization. I looked over at Marie again; tears were running down her cheeks. I reached for her hand, squeezing it tight. I could feel her trembling.

"We must get this jewel into the hands of the Grand Elder of the Synod. The Synod is in the pockets of Loath and Camio, but the Grand Elder believes in the old ways. He will fight to convict them of the highest crime. None of the members will challenge or sway him," explained Daevas.

"What about Camio?" questioned Preston.

"Camio and Loath, they're a package deal. Destroying one damages the other's position. The question is, who do we go after first? Puppet or Puppeteer?" Daevas paused to crack another beer. "If we can get the Elder on our side, we can build the case to shut down Camio before he can harvest Terra. For now, we have the element of surprise on our side. However, you must all remember that this is not a battle mission, this is infiltration. Be on your guard."

Daevas gestured us into a huddle, absently splashing his beer. "I know of a secret route into Araqiel's castle. Even *thinking* about calling it Loath's castle makes me sick. Although, I'm sure Loath had time to add his own bad taste to the décor," he grumbled, shaking his head. "Anyway. Once inside, we'll split into three groups. Marie, Nicole, and I will stall Loath. Tyler and Emily will get the jewel to the Elder in the eastern region of the castle. McKenzie and Preston will provide cover. If things get dicey, use the Wanderlust lockets to get out. Am I clear?"

I could tell from Marie and Nicole's expression's that there was no chance in hell they would just leave "if things got dicey." And Preston didn't seem thrilled to be on guard duty.

"Naturally dad's favorites get to have the fun," he mumbled.

"Favorites? You're joking, right?" snapped Nicole. "Maybe if you learned to be a stronger fighter."

"You, fight? More like flirt!"

The siblings' argument began to escalate.

"Hey!" shouted Daevas, "I don't give a rat's ass if anyone doesn't like the plan! Last I checked, none of ya has as many notches on your belts as me. So shut up, and let's get down to business! We start tomorrow at nightfall."

I sat outside on the steps with Marie and the others. I couldn't believe we had been up all night. As I reached my arm up to give my tired bones a stretch, I caught a glimpse of my watch face.

Six-thirty already! No wonder the birds are already singing.

This was actually it. I couldn't help but think about what was next for me. I'm sure if we succeeded, Marie would want to go home. I couldn't follow; my life was here. And aside from the unwanted Demon injection Nicole gave me, I was still a human at my core. I grabbed my jacket and began walking down the front steps.

"Ty's, where you going?" called Emily.

"Just going to get some air, is all," I replied.

I could hear Marie chasing after me – I would know the sound of her steps anywhere. I really just wanted a bit of me time. I needed to clear my head and possibly walk off a hangover. I just wasn't ready to look into those puppy dog eyes, nor was I prepared for this conversation. But as her insistent steps caught up to me, I knew she wouldn't accept my need for space. Everything was chess with Marie, and I wasn't ready to play.

She does this all the time. Pushing me into a corner like a raccoon fleeing an animal catcher. But am I any better? I bottle up feelings like tiny ships. Maybe it's time I change that.

"Sweets, what's wrong," Marie asked gently.

I couldn't hold back any longer. The last few months had been a rollercoaster of emotions, full of things I could never understand completely, even if I had been given two lifetimes to absorb them.

"I'll tell you what's wrong," I snapped. "If we succeed, that's it, you leave! You get your life back and I'm stuck here." I searched her eyes as my gaze hardened. "Are you going to take the kids?" My tone was rough, but I didn't care.

"Tyler, I—" Marie started, but I interrupted, letting my anger get the best of me.

"I wonder, Marie, was this your plan all along? Use me to fix these deeds, then it's home sweet home. Did you even really want me, all those years ago at that dumb party?"

Marie rolled her eyes, placing her hands on her hips. She sighed deeply, taking on the patience of a parent watching their child roll around in the midst of a tantrum.

"First of all: of course, I'll leave, for a little while. I haven't been home in ages. However, Sweets," she grabbed my hands and held them tenderly between us, "I want to stay here. This is my home now, here, with you and the kids. I'll always visit the place I'm from, but my home is here on Terra. And yes, sweets, that time way back when, I did want you. It wasn't until *weeks* later that I discovered your lineage, but by then it didn't matter one way or another. I was in love."

I felt my anger deflate. I had reacted out of fear, when I should have had more faith in us. Since Daevas' return, I honestly wanted this day to last forever. I had forgotten how much I actually enjoyed having all of us together. I knew they were different, and definitely odd, but they were my family. Marie jumped into my arms, wrapping me in a tight hug. I was never much of a hugger, and she was squeezing the life out of me like a boa constrictor. Upon her release, I let out a huge yawn. I was beat. I hadn't pulled an all-nighter since college.

"Hey Marie, why don't we leave the kids with your dad for a bit. Maybe you could teach me a few new spells or something. It might be useful later on," I suggested.

"Spells...Yeah, I'll teach you something, alright," winked Marie as she licked her lips, groping my butt as we walked back to the house.

As the day paced on, Marie's family and I did the most bizarre variety of tasks. We took turns resting, and prepared potions and elixirs. We looked at castle blueprints and played video games. The whole day was a strange mix of mission prepping and family time. Daevas was in rare form as well, tossing Logan into the air and teaching Harley how to use a sword – you know, typical grandpa stuff. He even offered to foot the bill for the castle roof. Then he showed off in the kitchen by preparing a lavish meal for us all. Later that evening, I dropped the kids off at my parents'. My parents had a knack for holding me hostage with conversation, and I was starting to run out of excuses to slip out.

By the time I got back to the castle it was time to go. I walked through the door and everyone was in Demon form, polishing their armor and weapons.

"Umm, what are you wearing, Tyler?" laughed Emily. "You're not going like that, are you?"

I looked down at my clothes. I mean, sure, it wasn't a shiny suit of armor like everyone else, but it's all I had. I guess a Star Wars shirt wouldn't be effective protection against a sword.

"Yeah sweets, you look like a dork," laughed Marie.

"What?! I always look like this!" I replied.

"Exactly," she chuckled.

"Hmm, she's right," grunted Daevas. "You won't be much good to us if you die within the first five minutes of the mission." He let out a big gravelly laugh. I found the prospect slightly less hilarious.

Daevas looked me up and down, and then pointed his large blade at my torso. The sword began to radiate a greenish hue.

Is he insane? He's not really going to blast me with that thing, is he?

Before I could protest, a ray of light struck my body and a whirlwind encircled me. I could feel my limbs being confined. The whipping air tightened around my form. As the whirlwind subsided, I was able to catch a glimpse of myself in our gothic-style mirror. I couldn't believe it: I was covered from head to toe in golden armor. My shoulders bore large golden epaulets, and across my back was draped a short purple cape. A black sash was wrapped around my waist, with a red tassel cascading down my thigh. My head was covered in a regal Viking-style helmet topped with two small golden horns. I could feel extra weight on my left arm. I was holding a small buckler shield engraved with some sort of weird calligraphy.

"That's more like it. Now you look like a proper soldier," grinned Daevas as he stroked his mustache.

I was ready. Well, maybe not totally ready, but there was no turning back now. It was midnight. We all gathered in the garden beneath a stain-glassed window at the back of the castle. I took one last deep breath, inhaling the heady scent of roses flowing over the chain link fence.

Daevas drew his blade and plunged it into the loose soil. He closed his eyes and began to chant slowly. I couldn't make out his words, it was some sort of Demonic language. I held Marie's hand, squeezing for dear life, sweaty palms hidden away inside my gauntlets. I was anxious as the stones behind us began to lift off of the ground and the air filled with static, forcing the hairs on my arms to stand up. A great beam of light broke through the night sky. I could feel the particles of my body dematerializing. I stared at my hand as it slowly turned into a pointillism painting. I caught a glimpse of the others. It didn't seem to bother them one bit; hell, Emily was examining her manicure through the transition.

Then, all at once we were standing in an empty field.

I could see the cattails from my first vision tilting softly in the breeze. It was warm, and two moons graced the night sky. Everything here was so quiet and different from my city norm, even the insects were not the same as the ones back on earth. Yet something about it felt familiar. It felt like home. A great shadow loomed over my shoulder in the moonlight. I turned to see the landscape tip up into a steep hill. Upon it stood a great castle towering in the moonlight, the color of alabaster. The moonlight was far brighter than the one on Terra, but it almost seemed to hide behind the castle, like a child leery of a stranger. Beneath the castle two waterfalls rushed out like infinite tears. It was almost poetic, hearing them crash against the rocks below. Golden gates surrounded the castle, with illuminated watchtowers on each side.

I was struck by the beauty and stood in speechless admiration. It was hard to think about anything else. Daevas was already speaking, telling us the main throne room was in the highest point of the tower. I wondered how we were going to get all the way up there unnoticed.

We trekked across the grassy field, avoiding contact with the patrolling guards. Daevas wasn't joking when he told us he had this all mapped out. Eventually we reached a great waterfall with a lock flowing inward below. As we jumped through the crashing waters, a gaping dark hole was revealed.

A strong sulfuric odor filled the air, burning the hair in my nostrils. Breathing was suddenly a great chore. It seemed as if the sewer went on for miles and miles. I feared that we would have to camp out in this horrible place. On top of everything else, it was dark, and my eyes were virtually useless, causing my other senses to go into overload. As if reading my mind, Marie created a ball of bright energy between her palms, then sent it bobbing along in the air in front of us.

Below our feet I could hear the waters swishing and swirling along the cobblestone path. Every so often I managed to catch a glimpse of a pink fin, followed by a grotesque groan in the distance. Not to mention the smell which differed from the sulfuric wind. This was the smell of dead flesh and rotting bone. Something was on our tail. Before we had a chance to react, a monster erupted from the sludgy waters. A large squid-like creature, it had eyes the size of truck tires and pale pink skin that reminded me of used chewing gum. The creature let out a phlegm-filled roar revealing rows upon rows of needle-like teeth.

"What the heck is that!" I screamed.

Marie used her magic to cast a detaining spell, stopping the creature in its tracks. I drew my blade and lunged at the beast. I was able to see his weak spot with Próvlepsi and severed one of its many arms. The power of Grus was astonishing. The monster groaned in extreme pain, flailing its oozing severed arm about, before retreating to the grimy waters and drifting away into the darkness.

"Seriously," I repeated, "What *was* that thing?"

"I bet these waterways inhabit many forms of Pooka. Most of them are probably hellbent on breaching the castle," said Preston.

"A pipe dream at best; the security within the castle is top-notch," replied Daevas.

I wondered if Daevas' play on words was intentional. I guess even Demon dads have terrible jokes. But I'll tell you what I didn't find funny -- how this made me feel about our chances of breaking in.

After a while of traveling the twists and turns of the grimy sewer system, we reached the lowest entrance of the castle.

"This is it," said Deavas. "Remember, no hero crap. Just stick to the plan."

Daevas opened the rusty gate, revealing an endless ladder stretching upward, a pinhole of light glimmering at its top. As we made the precipitous climb, I could feel my courage taking a backseat. With each clang of my metal boot my stomach twisted and turned. I was beyond nervous.

After what seemed like ages, we finally reached the top of the ladder. The others gracefully jumped out of the manhole on the castle floor, while I scuttled out like a shy turtle. My biceps and calves were burning from the workout and felt like jelly. When I finally looked up, I couldn't believe what I was looking at. If the outside had been any small indication of what was contained within, I still wasn't fully prepared. The place was more elegant than I ever could have imagined, with white marble floors and large pillars leading to the ornately painted ceiling. The ceiling was covered with elaborate pictures of Angels and Demons in front of a beautiful skyline. Hovering above them were ten mysterious figures. I had never been to the Sistine Chapel, but this place made it look like a cheap coloring book.

Purples and reds glimmered in the moonlit stained-glass windows.

A series of large statues ran parallel down each side of the hall. If I was a betting man, I would say these were famous kings and warriors. I was blown away by the technology within the castle. Holograms and digital photos were projected throughout the foyer. Small robots roamed the main floor polishing the marble to a mirror finish; it was the perfect blend of technology and Hellenistic art.

"Alright, everyone, just up the hall are the warp elevators. I can hack one to take us to our stops." Marie began to break down our objectives for each floor. "Level twenty-one, that's the guard station. Preston, Mckenzie, that's you. Stay out of sight and keep us posted on their movements. Level thirty, that's where the Grand Elder resides, his chamber should be in the far east wing. Tyler, Emily, get the jewel to the Elder, try to avoid confrontation if possible. Nicole, dad, and I will go to the throne room on the fiftieth floor. We'll keep Loath off your back and give you time with the Elder. Everyone clear?"

The elevator ride gave me vertical whiplash, with my lunch rising to my mouth like an astronaut in a space simulator. We were five floors away from my stop and I was running out of time. I swallowed my refunded Cheerios and turned to Marie. I had grand plans to say something important or meaningful, but instead I stuttered some kind of nonsense. I got two-and-a-half words out when Marie placed her finger on my lips and shook her head.

"Don't say it, sweets. Just come back to me, okay?" she whispered. She gave me a tight hug and affectionately brushed some grime from my cheek.

Emily and I got off the elevator and the doors shut in what seemed like slow motion. I could feel my heart skip a beat, watching Marie's face disappear through the tiny crack of the elevator. I was left with my reflection in the elevator door. I looked at myself, and all I could think was how far I had come. I knew I was more than a warrior, more than a Merozantine, I was good ol' Tyler Pine from Terra, and I was happy with that.

Maybe I'm finally becoming the man I should be, I thought.

Emily and I dashed through the East Wing of the castle. It didn't take long before we tripped security. We were confronted by three armored angels, all draped from head to toe in swanky gold-colored armor and wielding lances. Before we knew it, we were locked in combat, forced to lay waste to a pack of Loath's goons. We were so close, our goal merely a few feet away.

As we approached the chamber of the Grand Elder, my heart began to pound. We stood in front of two towering wooden doors. I reached for the intricate silver door handles, two carved serpents woven together, but before I had a chance to pull, a mysterious figure emerged from the chamber doorway. I couldn't help but feel that I had met this man before.

"Oh God no, it can't be," grimaced Emily.

I knew exactly who it was, but I had to be sure. "Emily, who is this guy? Do you know him?" I asked.

"Yeah, Ty's, this is Camio, former Grand Marshal of Empyrean. Now, King of Gauguin." She spat these last words like they were poison to her.

"Out of our way!" I shouted. "We have no time for nonsense!"

Camio pushed his round glasses higher onto the bridge of his nose. He adjusted his regal white gloves, before rolling up his sleeves, which looked like dragon scales. I could feel the power emanating from his body. He was definitely the guy from my visions, but something was different about him.

"Get out of our way, you monster!" shouted Emily, as she charged for a magic blast.

"Spare me," Camio murmured. "I wouldn't try that if I were you."

Emily shot at him anyway. He deflected the blast with a wave of a hand, as if it were an insect in the air. The blast bounced off of his fingertips and blew a hole through a nearby wall.

"Come now, you certainly must feel it, T. We are bound together," Camio whispered to me telepathically.

His voice alone caused me to shudder. I knew what I had to do; I just didn't know how to do it. I raised my hand, halting Emily's assault. This was my fight, not hers.

"How did you know we were coming?" I said aloud.

Camio's voice shot through my brain. *"That sword you have is linked to me and to your forefathers. Upon its re-forging, our bond was once again complete. I must say I'm impressed by you; you've certainly forced my hand. Bravo, Merozantine."*

Camio removed his large cloak, revealing the legendary Byzantine sword in his hand. He attempted to strike, but I had drawn Grus and was ready to deflect his assault. Camio's speed and agility was astonishing, but I was able to keep up. I kicked it up a level by unlocking my Demon form.

Camio swiftly drew a sort of pentagram symbol in the air, shooting the five-point magic star in my direction. It felt as if my body was moving in slow motion. Camio managed to knock Grus from my hands, placing his blade upon my neck with a fencer's sophistication.

"You can't run from your destiny, Tyler Pine," whispered Camio. "It was written by my hand long ago, that our fates are to be forever intertwined."

"I don't care about any bond between us. Once the Grand Elder sees this footage of your lapdog's massacre, you and Loath are finished."

"Finished? But this is just the beginning for you and I."

Camio removed his saber from my quivering throat, placing it back into its scabbard. He raised his hand and created an energy ball, twisting and gradually shaping its structure into a black gate.

"You've come a long way. Do what you must, but it won't stop the inevitable. The bloodline of the Mammon will flow through the cosmos."

The Mammon? What the heck is that, I pondered. *No one had ever mentioned a Mammon to me.*

"We are the mirror image to the Seraphs, the shadow to the light."

Seraphs? Wait, who are they? I thought. *I have the feeling there's more here that I haven't been told.*

"Unlike other Demons, my greatest strength is my ability to absorb power. As you'll learn, to obtain power one must make sacrifices. Meridian has the ability to control time. A very useful skill, that serves a greater good within my being. With his power now mine, I am the closest thing to a God."

I looked over at Emily and saw the fear in her eyes. A guy like this, with the power of a God, was bad news for not only us but for the flow of time itself. I felt the same helplessness that I had become so used to feeling since this all began. It was infuriating, and most of all, I hated feeling afraid when I knew I had a family relying on me.

"Stopping me here only prolongs fate elsewhere. I will harvest the souls of Terra and power the cannon, when and where I see fit," said Camio. I couldn't help feeling that I was one step behind. "This timeline is yours...for now." He gestured with his hand, opening the black gate. "Don't feel discouraged, our paths are destined to cross again."

Camio glided past Emily and me and through the gate, which closed in on itself and disappeared. We were alone outside the chamber once more. I placed my blade into its sheath and dropped my shield, the crash echoing across the marble floor. I was being forced to come to terms with what this all meant for me, and my role in this battle. When the time came, could I really stop Camio? I had gotten it wrong. The vision -- I must have missed something. Was this part of his plan the whole time? How could we ever stop him if he could travel through time? And who were the Mammon, exactly?

My frustration bubbling up, I looked at Emily in anguish. "How could I have let this happen? This isn't fair! He should have to pay for his crimes! Now he gets to just walk away. And then what? Another parallel universe pays the price?"

"Take it easy on yourself, there's no way you could have predicted this," said Emily. "And as furious as I am about this new development, we need to secure victory here if we can. The fact that he went to drastic measures to fuse with Meridian means he's desperate. Let's get this to the Elder and save our kingdom."

Emily and I cautiously entered the chamber of the Elder. The room was dimly lit with melting candles which covered every nook and cranny. It resembled a monk's chamber: steam was swirling over a small koi pond in the center of the chamber, with three planks hovering above as if held by invisible hands. I couldn't believe my eyes. It was The Grand Elder, a shriveled old man the size of a small teddy bear. To be honest, I was expecting something a little more intimidating.

The little creature squinted as he looked up from a thick and dog-eared tome.

"Hello, Grand Elder. I am Tyler of Terra. We wish to have an audience with--"

I glanced at Emily and saw that she had taken a knee, as if she was proposing. In our haste to leave Terra, no one took the time to school me on the customs in this realm.

"Psst, Tyler, what are you doing, kneel!" whispered Emily, as if I was supposed to magically *know* that. I stifled an eye roll and dropped to one knee.

"Grand Elder. If I may have a word, I would like to present to you this piece of crucial evidence regarding the slaughter of innocent Demons under the ruling of King Araqiel II." I held out the jewel but received no response from the small creature. How long was he just going to sit there with a blank expression on his face? Suddenly a deep voice echoed throughout the chamber.

"You are a Merozantine, are you not?" the teddy bear asked in his oddly incongruous voice. "I was under the impression that you were all but extinct. Yet here you are. Very interesting!" he said, looking me over from head to toe. "Ahh, I see you have a Parroting Crystal. Oh my, I haven't seen one of those in ages." He chuckled excitedly. He hopped down from his chair and scampered up to me, his head only coming to my knee. He peered curiously at the crystal, reminding me of a chipmunk examining an acorn.

"This is astonishing, and it's in mint condition!" the little guy said. "It's beautifully cut; it even has the original chain! How did someone so young obtain one of these?"

"Sir, if I may," interjected Emily. "We are on a bit of a time crunch. We humbly ask that you review the contents of the Crystal. We believe that Loath, King of Dada, is responsible for the countless murders of innocent Demons. I ask that..."

The elder raised his tiny wrinkled hand, halting Emily in the middle of her speech.

"Ahh, Loath," sighed the Elder. "How could someone so talented, so special and unique, be filled with such rage and hate. Since his youth, I've tried time and time again to guide him. I only wished to ease his anger and hatred, but he could never be swayed. This allegation doesn't shock me. I've always known that one day his rage would get the best of him. His animosity toward Demons stems from loss, you know."

"Loss? What do you mean?" I replied.

"When he was very young, Loath lost his mother. She was a brave warrior and a protector of the King. She was killed during an assassination attempt, during the early days of the kingdom when Demons and Angels were still at odds. An assassin tried to murder the king during a treaty dinner. Loath's mother put her life on the line, saving him from a poison arrow." He paused and hung his head in sorrow. "It was rumored that the killer was a Demon. As a boy, Loath couldn't understand that one Demon doesn't represent the entire race. This revenge fueled him, poor child. But do not misunderstand me: there is no excuse for the slaughter of the innocent."

The Elder sighed deeply. I could tell by his tone that he truly cared for Loath.

"I will see that this matter is resolved and bring justice to the Kingdom and its former King," said the Elder gravely.

Emily and I rose to our feet and thanked the Grand Elder for his time. We hoped that with his power and wisdom he could right one of so many wrongs within the kingdom.

"Well, Ty's, we did it," shouted Emily with glee. But her excitement was brief. "We need to get going. I feel like we're needed elsewhere."

I just prayed Marie and the others had been successful. I was positive that Loath wouldn't surrender quietly.

X
Grey Matters

Emily and I left the Grand Elder and planned to join up with Marie, Nicole, and Daevas. They were just outside the doors of the throne room, and we ran to join them.

"Sweets, you're okay, thank goodness!" shouted Marie, wrapping her wings around me as she hugged me tight.

"Oh, hey Marie, glad to see you, too," said Emily sarcastically.

"Enough banter!" shouted Daevas. "This is important. Did you two get the message to the elder?"

"Yeah, so--" I started to speak, but Emily butted in.

"We got it to him, dad, but not before we ran into Camio,"

"Camio? Here? Damn, we better move our asses. Camio and Loath may prove to be too much to handle together," said Daevas.

"Well, Camio is gone, actually. I think we're in the clear," I said.

"Gone?" shouted Daevas, snapping his head in my direction. "Well, either way, we don't have time for this horse crap. Let's get a move on."

As we stepped into the room, I momentarily forgot about everything as I took in the imposing beauty of the room. The girls walked ahead as Daevas launched into Tour Guide Dad Mode, giving a detailed history lesson about the room, the castle history, and its kings. I stole a glance at Marie, who was rolling her eyes and stifling a yawn. Nicole was drawing in patience with a deep breath, feigning interest as Daevas lectured on -- I could tell they had heard this story many times before.

As for me, I hardly knew where to look first. The Throne Room was a grand and exquisite place. The walls were covered with gold Angelic and Demonic hieroglyphs, shimmering in the moonlight. Some of the hieroglyphs moved as we passed, reminding me of those cool 3D art puzzles from the nineties. The black marble floor was flecked with gold. High above our heads hung a grand chandelier, and rows of massive black columns lined either side of the room. An intricate stained-glass window made up the back wall, depicting the chronology of Empyrean.

The room's best feature was the throne itself. A massive golden chair, each armrest was made of obsidian, carved into the likeness of a Demon and an Angel. Rubies glittered in the eye sockets. It was all much richer in every way than anything I had ever encountered. Hell, the satin cushion looked so luxurious, I bet if I had tried to sit in it, it would have ejected me onto the floor. However, I knew that now wasn't the time to be smitten by a room.

"Come out, Loath," shouted Daevas. "There's nowhere left to hide. It's time to atone!"

I could hear the barely contained rage in my father-in-law's voice. I felt lucky that he had always liked me; I did not want to be on the wrong side of him. In this case, I knew his rage was justified. Daevas needed to get even for everything he had suffered as a result of Loath and Camio's plans. This wasn't just a matter of pride. This was about honor and vindication.

"You and Camio have made a mockery of the kingdom for long enough. It's time to set things right." A tall blonde figure appeared from behind the throne. It was Loath. Daevas set his jaw, his daughters drawing their weapons behind him – Daevas' most loyal knights. I took a big gulp of air, trying my best to keep my composure.

The Angel's arrogance oozed through his entire being, even manifesting in the clothes he wore. His golden armor was over-the-top and gaudy: bright shoulder pads like something from an eighties soap opera, a long flowing cape, and Araqiel's crown. It was the very symbol Daevas had sworn to protect, the ultimate insult on the head of this two-faced fraud.

"My, my, Daevas," said Loath. "I must say, I'm shocked to see you in such good health."

Daevas glared at him in disgust. The two locked eyes. The stink of hatred wafted in the air.

"I, Daevas of the Ashi, leader of the Knights of the Sistine Madonna, defender of the crown, am here to bring you to justice. You have committed mass murder. If you surrender now, your execution will be fair and swift," Daevas roared, gripping his blade as if punctuating his sentence. "Will you go quietly, or will I have to use force? The evidence is already with the Grand Elder."

"That tiny old fool?" chuckled Loath. "I assure you, nothing you do or say could possibly sway my Synod."

I couldn't believe this guy; he acted as though the Synod was his personal lap dog.

Daevas lowered his head, furrowing his brow. Loath smiled deviously, settling into his presumed win.

"I understand, sir. But how would you explain this to *your* Synod?" said Daevas, extending his hand to reveal a Windfall stone. It was a copy of the footage we had given to the Elder. A beam shot up, illuminating the room with a glowing blue hologram. The terrible footage played silently.

"Women, children, men, all cut down like stalks of wheat in a field. And you bathing in the blood of the innocent, laughing hysterically. Sickening." Daevas glared at him in grim satisfaction. "This is the end of the line, Loath."

Loath's face fell and he grew even paler than normal. "What... where... how did you get that?" he stuttered. He backed away, as though physically distancing himself from the film would undo the evidence on it. "Tell me, where did you get that from?!"

"Where we got it from is irrelevant, you jerk," shouted Marie. "It's over."

Loath turned purple with rage. "It doesn't matter!" he screamed. "You will all soon be dead, and when I'm through with you, I'll strangle that little Elder! This is my kingdom, and no vile Demon will take it from me. I won't tolerate it! I'll send for Camio; he won't allow you to upend our plans!"

"Sorry friend, Camio doesn't care about your interests. He never has," Nicole replied, smiling. "He's going to destroy you and your half of the kingdom with the Durendal Cannon. Your plans never mattered to him. You were just a chess piece."

Sweat coated Loath's forehead. He looked helpless.

"Loath," Daevas said calmly, "Surrender."

"Never," whispered the Angel, glowering with rage. In a last desperate act, he drew his blade and charged at Daevas.

The two began to battle in the middle of the throne room. The impact of each clash began to crack and crumble the room. Loath took to the air, momentarily confusing Daevas and knocking his blade out of his hand. What began as a duel, now devolved into a brawl. Daevas used his telekinesis to hurl chunks of rubble at his opponent, knocking Loath's sword from his hand. Loath countered with interstellar energy blasts, turning the rubble into particles.

We watched from the side, tense and agitated.

"Should we help him?" I asked, looking to Daevas' daughters for a clue.

"That's it, I'm jumping in," shouted Nicole, bolstered by my question.

"No!" said Marie, looking at Nicole, then at me. "Dad would never forgive you if you interfered. This is not our battle."

Daevas and Loath began to grapple in mid-air, slamming each other into the walls of the room and leaving small craters. They broke apart momentarily. Loath conjured a ball of energy, blasting Daevas directly in the face and sending him hurtling across the room. Daevas managed to regain his footing, and lunged forward, leading with his massive fist, which was engulfed in flames. He made contact with Loath's stomach, forcing him to double over and singeing his armor.

What a rumble, I thought. *I wouldn't have guessed in a million years that the old Dave I knew, the big softy who shed tears at our wedding, could throw down like this!*

As Daevas geared up for another round, Loath opened his mouth and let out a screeching high note, piercing our ears. In response, the walls and floor began to crack apart like eggshells.

"Agh, what the heck is this!" shouted Marie, clapping her hands over her ears. The screech brought us all to our knees.

"It's like nails on a chalkboard!" screamed Emily.

Loath quickly dashed to his fallen rapier, keen to have the upper hand.

"Dad! Heads up!" shouted Marie as she flung Daevas his saber.

Daevas reached out to catch the blade, but it was too late. Just as his hand curled around the hilt, Loath jabbed his épée into Daevas' side, bringing him to his knees.

Pale with worry, Nicole and Emily dashed to Daevas' aid.

Seeing her father injured was too much for Marie to handle – she began to lose control, transforming into her Max Demon mode. I knew Marie couldn't maintain this state, and I wasn't sure how long she was going to last against power like Loath's. I was frozen with fear and indecision. I watched as she ran to pick up her father's blade, just in time to clash swords with Loath. Nicole and Emily administered healing magic to their father's wound as Marie fought with Loath. They matched each other in speed and power, locking blades, testing each other's limits. Marie was practically glowing, moving efficiently like a perfectly engineered machine with each parry and thrust. Watching her and Loath face off against each other, I was witnessing an opera of chaos – beautiful and frightening.

"You are indeed a skilled opponent. But not skilled enough," said Loath, panting, as sparks sizzled across their swords. "I'll be sure to slaughter everything you love, once I dispose of your washed-up father!" He pushed off of Marie's blade with his, forcing her back. Marie nearly toppled but regained her footing and dashed toward Loath in a furious rage, aiming her blade at his chest. Loath held his blade out in front of him.

The two ran toward each other until they were inches apart, moving so quickly that for a moment, I didn't know what had happened.

Blood dripped onto the floor between their feet. Loath's blade had run Marie through, the tip glinting where it had torn through her back.

"I told you, little girl," said Loath. "You're not worthy of this fight!"

He wrapped his arm around her waist, pulling her body into him, toward the hilt of his blade. She gasped as tears sprung to her eyes. It was a tiny, strangled cry, a sound so vulnerable that for a moment I didn't understand that it was coming from the fearless woman I knew.

"No! No! Stop!" I shouted, feeling the stupid words tumble out of my mouth, as I dropped to my knees, helpless.

Loath ripped his blade from Marie's body and swung her toward me with one arm. She spilled onto the floor. The thud of her body against the marble was sickening. Emily ran to her.

I go to my feet, drawing Grus. I only had revenge on my mind.

As I charged at Loath, I knew two things more clearly than ever before: I loved Marie with all of my heart; and I had to wipe the stain of this bastard from existence. I raised Grus and swung it at Loath's scalp, just as a large circle of light appeared between us. A familiar face stepped out of the beaming ring.

It was Flower.

My fight was not with him. I halted my blade, stepping back. Realizing my face was streaming with tears I hastily swiped at my cheek.

"Perfect timing!" shouted Loath triumphantly.

Flower looked at him impassively and produced a long-stemmed white rose. He manipulated and twisted it until it transformed into a flintlock. Stretching out an elegant arm, he cocked it and pointed it at my forehead. I was inches away, but I was unafraid. My life and death no longer mattered. I only had to make Loath pay.

"Get out of my way, Flower," I ordered, my Demon blood percolating in my veins.

"Well?" Loath's tone changed to irritation. "It's about time someone showed up to assist me. Now be a good girl, boy, whatever you are and finish this worm."

The Flower locked eyes with me, his finger resting lightly on the trigger. I couldn't make a move – I couldn't avenge Marie if I was killed before I could raise my sword. I felt so useless. Out of the corner of my eye, I could see her prone body in Emily's arms; Emily was muttering incantations in a shaky voice. *God, please let her live,*

I thought, fresh tears running down my face.

"What are you waiting for, idiot?" barked Loath. "Finish him! KILL HIM!"

The Flower turned to Loath with the flintlock, touching it to the Angel's forehead. He pulled the trigger, blasting a seed bullet right between Loath's eyes. A fine red mist cut through the air, spraying Flower's pale arm, as Loath's body fell back. It landed at the foot of the throne, blood and grey matter spattered across the black marble beyond him.

For a moment, everything in my head went completely silent. It was like everyone else had disappeared. The edges of my vision went black. As Loath lay on the ground, a rivulet of blood trickled down his face. His jaw was slack, lips parted, as if still trying to get the last word.

I stared at Flower in disbelief. He stood there, looking stern but otherwise composed, staring in vague dismay at the blood droplets on his arm. One bright red splotch was on his cheek, but he seemed not to notice or care.

If Flower was willing to turn on his leader, what did that mean for us? Nicole and Emily were huddled around Marie, ready to sacrifice their own lives for their sister.

The Flower raised his flintlock, pointing at me once more. The vines retracted, the pistol reverting to a rose. I breathed out all at once, wondering how long I had been holding my breath through all of this.

"I remember the day we came across that village," the Flower started. "In all my years of service to the Kingdom, I had seen nothing like it. You couldn't possibly fathom it -- seeing children lying prone with wide open eyes, as if they were watching their own souls drift into the ether." He paused then, a darkness seeming to flit across his fine features like a sudden storm cloud blocking the sun. "It took some time for me to break free of Camio's control, and even more time to build up the courage to do what was necessary."

I was perplexed. Did this mean he was on our side now? What was coming next? Briefly, I placed my hand on my sword, then allowed it to drop.

The bloom has not gone off of you just yet, Tyler,» said Flower, as he sniffed the white rose in his hand. He glanced at Loath, then tossed the rose carelessly onto his corpse. "Consider this a truce. I no longer have any interest in harming you. My enemy is Camio." The Madonna snapped his fingers, vanishing into a portal of light. I drew in a breath and stepped away from the body, bringing my attention back to the most important thing.

Marie.

The look on Emily and Nicole's faces told me that Marie was not healing. I pushed past them to join her. She was losing a lot of blood. I scooped her into my arms, brushing dirt off of her cheek.

"Nicole, do something, heal her!" I shouted. "Use your magic, or a potion!"

"I'm sorry, Tyler, I've tried everything," cried Nicole, tears running down her face.

"No, no, I don't believe you! Marie, please just hang on," I cried.

Daevas joined his injured daughter, clutching his side. I could hear a ding beyond the throne room. I hoped it was McKenzie and Preston getting off the elevator.

Daevas was a mess. I couldn't look at him; I had never seen him cry before, and I didn't want to. Marie pulled me close with what little strength she had left, struggling to wipe the tears from my eyes.

"Hey Sweets," she whispered softly. "I think I may have overreacted a bit. Oops." She tried to chuckle but broke into a coughing fit.

There was blood on her lips.

"Try not to talk, Marie, save your strength," I said, sniffing back snot and tears. I was a total wreck.

"God, sweets, you love a good cliché," she joked with tears in her eyes. "I know this whole ordeal has been hard on you. Listen," she said, placing her hand on mine. It already felt so cold. "I need you to promise me you'll be happy. And please, take good care of the kids. Teach them about love… the way you taught me."

I held Marie close and kissed her bloodied lips. She was struggling to breathe now, and her body felt so small as I squeezed her tight. Even in her last breaths, I couldn't believe how beautiful she was.

Marie's body began to glow, shimmering gold rays illuminating her from within. It became brighter and brighter. She slowly vanished into nothing, leaving me holding only her armor, which collapsed in on itself and clattered to the ground.

I doubled over until my forehead was pressed against the cold marble, choking on my tears. I was alone, the kids were motherless; what was I going to do?

Marie's family held each other, a river of tears. Daevas laid his hands on my shoulders, offering me empty consolations. He didn't believe the words coming out of his mouth any more than I did.

The six of us left the castle, devastated. We had won the battle, but victory had never felt so meaningless.

* * *

Being in this world felt strange, especially without the comforting anchor of having Marie at my side. The warm dry days sometimes made it feel like being on a vacation, but with a gaping hole next to me instead of the woman I loved the most. I drifted through the days and nights without any real sense of time or place.

Maries family pretty much owned Oldenburg, so it was easy for them to get me a room in one of its finest inns in town. The kids had their own room next door. The inn had a very mom-and-pop feel, with a wraparound porch on which a makeshift swing dangled. Most of my time was spent either curled up in my room in bed, numb and heartbroken, or on the porch swing, nursing my sorrows with a drink.

It was nearly noon as I rocked back and forth, hypnotizing myself with the motion, sipping a glass of Demon whiskey. My eyes were bloodshot; blinking became a hell of a chore. I had cried so much that my tear ducts had dried up like an old well. Inside the inn, someone was frying something up; the smell was drifting out onto the porch as I struggled to remember the last thing I ate, and when. I yearned for a bite, but through an open window, I heard other people talking and chuckling in the dining room. I didn't want to face any-one, so I stayed on the swing, listening to my stomach groan.

Damn it, if Marie was here, she would tell me to grow a pair and go in. But I don't need pity, I've been getting enough of that all week.

I thought back, as I had countless times that week, on the day Ma-rie died, and everything that had happened inside that room. Maybe it was my Demon blood talking, but I was furious. I wanted that kill, and Flower took it from me. I should have been the one to tear Loath to pieces for what he did to my family.

I knew Marie wouldn't want me thinking like that, so I tried vainly to quell my rage. I wondered for a moment if my life was worth any-thing anymore, with her gone. But I knew the kids would need me. They would be all alone if anything happened to me. I couldn't bear to even look at their heartbroken little faces – I had been avoiding them the entire time we had been in Oldenburg. I was grateful that their aunts had taken turns doting on them, making sure they were being fed and bathed and put to bed at a reasonable hour, since I could barely do any of that for myself.

I swirled the final drop of whiskey before tossing it back, fresh tears forming in the corners of my eyes.

"Hey, Ty's," whispered a gentle voice behind me.

It was Emily. Hurriedly, I wiped my eyes onto my sleeve.

"Oh hey Em, whats up?" I sniffed, clearing my throat.

Emily had been pretty much taking care of me through all of this, doing everything possible to keep my spirits up. Heck, she was even going to earth every morning to get me coffee from my favorite spot.

"Got you your favorite, Ty. Extra tall vanilla cold brew, no whipped cream."

"Thanks, Emily," I replied, taking a tiny sip. "You know, you don't need to keep doing this." It was extremely kind of her, but honestly, nothing tasted the same anymore. I only wanted one taste, Marie's lips gently pecking my own in the morning.

"Look, Ty's, I have an idea. Everyone's going to lunch at the place down the street in a few, just for a change of pace and to clear our heads a little. You really should come with. Besides, I bet a nice big meal would make you feel better."

"Thanks for the invite, Em. But I think I just want to be by myself for a bit. I'm just not up to it. Is that okay?"

"Of course. Take your time, Tyler. When you're ready, we'll chat, okay? We'll all get through this. Just try to take care of yourself," she said before giving me a gentle hug.

Take care of myself, yeah right. I was doing a bang-up job so far. I hadn't even figured out what I was going to tell my parents. How was I supposed to take care of two children myself? I was sure I had lost my job by now, but it didn't matter to me. I was awaiting my wife's funeral. I had been a zombie in mourning, going through the motions of my day-to-day, and alternating between numbing my grief and being consumed by it. I knew that I was the world's worst father right now, but even that felt miles away from me right now.

Later that night the inhabitants of Oldenburg gathered Marie's armor and placed it in a roaring fire. They melted it down and formed it into pieces of jewelry just for us, Marie's closest surviving relatives.

"You, come forward," the Grand Elder requested, gesturing toward McKenzie.

Mckenzie sobbed openly as she approached to open an elaborately carved box lined with yellow silk.

"Wow… look at these," said McKenzie through her tears. The people gathered craned their necks to see what the pieces looked like.

"They're bracelets!" shouted McKenzie, taking one and holding it up for us all to see.

I approached the box to observe the gifts and marvel at their beauty. It was unsurprising to me that Demons were known for their smelting skills. This jewelry had no equal with anything I had ever seen on earth. Each bracelet was engraved with Marie's name in Demonic script. The gold was lightweight and shimmered as it was turned. Each one held a small purple jewel. I fought back my tears as I admired them. But I couldn't help but notice there were only seven. Marie's father, her siblings, and our children were accounted for. So where was mine? Maybe I hadn't gotten one because I was still a human, even with Demon blood flowing in my veins. I tried not to show that I was hurt. The grief over Marie's death was bigger than my feelings of being shut out.

For the remainder of the night, I hid from most of the crowds. I set up camp behind the inn, staring at the stars from a wooden crate for a seat.

"Ahh, here you are, Merozantine! I've been looking for you," said a crackly voice behind me. It was the Grand Elder

"Young man, I am terribly sorry for your loss," he said, lowering his teddy-bear-like head. "But I'm sure you're tired of hearing that." He gazed thoughtfully at the stars, silent a moment. When he spoke again, it was to address the very thing I was trying not to think about. "My, those bracelets are beautiful, don't you think?" I said nothing. He continued on as though he did not notice. "Demons, despite what some may like you to think, are a very generous breed."

The Elder hopped onto a crate coming to eye level with me. He raised his small paw, materializing a sword sheath out of thin air.

"What's this," I asked, speaking for the first time since he had appeared. I looked at the seemingly ordinary sheath.

"It is customary to provide a grief-stricken family with aid. And if I>m not mistaken, you didn>t receive a bracelet."

"Thanks, Grand Elder," I said, taking the sheath. "I guess it's better to keep Grus protected and clean, right," I added, looking at the gift, still not quite understanding his motivations.

"Well Tyler, this sheath does more than protect Grus. But for now, I will refrain from saying more. Just know this sheath will take you where you need to go, my boy," the Elder grinned conspiratorially, before tottering away.

Where I needed to go? What did that mean? I mused on this for a moment and then found my mind wandering. It was increasingly difficult to concentrate on anything anymore. I just wished I had Marie back.

Maybe Emily was right about inviting me to lunch. I *did* need to get out of my head, vent to somebody a little bit, let my emotions run their course. This was a task I usually reserved for Justin, when

Marie used to get on my nerves. It felt like Justin and I hadn't seen each other in ages. *When was the last time we talked, anyway? That day on campus, when he was vying for that job,* I thought guiltily.

I had been such a selfish friend. I hadn't even reached out to see how the interview had gone. Justin had always understood me, though, and always had my back when I needed it. Maybe it was time I pulled him into the loop.

Reaching into my pocket, I removed a Windfall stone and started recording my whole story, from start to finish.

Over two hours later, I finished. I had laughed, yelled, and cried through my narration and now I was ready to share it with my best friend. Now I just had to get it to him.

I popped open a Wanderlust locket, the one that belonged to Marie. I couldn't believe I was able to control it, but the effort and work it had taken me to harness my Demon blood and not let it run me ended up helping in more ways than I could have predicted. Through the shimmering portal, I could see Justin's room. I grabbed the Windfall stone and tossed it in as hard as I could. I just hoped he would find it soon. I needed a conversation with an actual human to balance me out a little.

The next day, the town celebrated Marie's life with a big festival. There were plenty of weird foods, from slimy squid-like platters to giant Demon-shaped cookies. They also engaged in carnival-like games much different than the ones on Terra. Everything from Fireball Toss to Hover the Boulder, and of course, plenty of drinking accompanied every activity.

In the main dining hall, Marie's father and siblings sat around a table exchanging stories with friends and relations. The tales were filled with plenty of laughs and tears. McKenzie told a story about how Marie once beat up Preston and in retaliation, he chased her around with a large club until she flew into a tree and sat there until nightfall, when he finally got bored and went back home. Emily told us about the time Marie blew up Daevas' weapon room in a bid to mix a better potion than Nicole, a story that caused Daevas to roar with laughter, tears in his eyes. "You can laugh now, huh, Dad? Only took two centuries for you to get over it," Emily teased. Nicole talked about how great of a mother Marie was, and how much she spoiled Harley, arguably the first Demon to put Hello Kitty stickers on her wings.

I turned to glance outside, where Harley and Logan were running in circles around a tree, play-fighting with sticks. When we first arrived at Oldenburg, I had wondered how I would tell the kids about their mom. This was the hardest emotional trial of my life and I couldn't imagine trying to struggle through being a proper father to two grieving children. But on the same night we arrived, I overheard McKenzie talking to the children in a low and gentle voice. I had crept out of my room and watched through the crack in their door. I strained to listen in.

"Harley, Logan, I want you two to be very good for your father," McKenzie was saying in a gentle voice. "Your mommy is gone, but we are going to keep her in our hearts, right?" I watched Harley and Logan nodding, tears on their soft cheeks. I marveled at how little they still were, and how underneath all the tantrums and mayhem, they carried a wisdom that I knew they could have only gotten from their mother.

"Just remember," McKenzie said, squeezing their hands, "She loved you both more that anything in the universe."

I just didn't have the heart to keep listening and hurried back to my room before anyone saw me in the hallway. I was moved to tears by McKenzie's kindness in handling the situation. I appreciated it more than I had the words or the heart to say.

My mind drifted back into the room as the family erupted into laughter, remembering another hilarious story about Marie. I stood and headed for the door. I needed some air. Insects were chirping in the still air of the late afternoon. I could feel another crying session bubbling up as I watched my children sitting in the grass, plucking at the blades and talking quietly to each other.

The thud of footfalls behind me alerted me to my brother-in-law.

"Hey bro, you okay out here?" asked Preston gently.

"Yeah… yeah, I'm fine," I replied, both of us fully aware that I wasn't.

"I get it," said Preston. I could tell he wanted to say more, but what was there to say? He rested his large hand on my shoulder. We both stared at the ground. I kicked at a pebble with my toe, suddenly feeling very much like a kid again, ill-equipped at dealing with tragedy, with responsibility. I wanted to run away.

"Hey, P. I'm gonna take a walk, can you watch the kids for me?"

Preston simply gave a nod, happy to have something to occupy his thoughts. This was uniquely devastating for each of us.

For a while, I aimlessly walked through the town, until I reached a large grassy hill covered in cattail reeds. It was so peaceful and reminded me of the vision Marie had showed me the first time I discovered who she really was. It felt like forever ago. I took a deep breath and stared up at the sky, slowing turning from pink to gold, hinting at the approach of twilight. All I could think about was her. I could still feel her brushing the dirt from my cheek, could see her gentle smile and feel the way it made my heart skip a beat. But my moment of serenity was interrupted when I felt someone watching me. I turned and spotted two figures standing at the top of the hill. I wondered how long they had been there.

Feeling reckless, I strode through the cattails directly at them. I knew who it was before I was even halfway there. I knew that things weren't what they seemed that day. It had been just a little bit too effortless, defeating her.

"Hello, Tyler," said the Wolf from beneath a mask carved from walnut. The black knight who I had watched kill her stood off to the side, unmoving. I quickly placed my hand on the hilt of my sword.

"That won't be necessary," said the Wolf. "Battle is not what brings us here." She paused. The wind whistled through the reeds behind me. "I wish to enlist your services."

"You want my services?" I gave a mirthless laugh. "Forgive me for not jumping at the opportunity. Now, if you'll excuse me." I turned my back on the duo and briskly began to make my way down the hillside, my heart pounding angrily.

"What if I told you that I could bring Marie back?"

I stopped in my tracks. I turned around and looked at the Wolf with fire in my eyes.

"Don't you ever mention her damn name! You don't get that privilege, understand?" I turned my back once more to depart.

"You think that this just ends here?" shouted the Wolf, "Don't be foolish, Tyler, you know just as well as I do that you have unfinished business with Camio."

I was furious, and yet I was desperate. Her offer was working its way into my grief, seducing me. I would have been willing to try anything. But to achieve it by placing my trust in Wolf seemed like a mistake.

"Are you familiar with the Mammon?" asked Wolf.

She knew that she had my attention. And something else was now happening. The landscape dropped out of my view, replacing it with a dense fog. I could feel the Wolf in my mind, projecting a vision.

The fog cleared away, and I could see the Old Gods creating the Ser-

aph and the Mammon to serve the Angels and Demons. But eventually, the power of these two beings intimidated the Gods. Only one of these creatures could be allowed to exist: The Seraph. Yet, the Mammon was too strong and would not allow itself to be extinguished so easily, so the Gods forced the Seraph to absorb the Mammon's energy, locking it away forever in a Dark Realm.

I saw the Wolf, the Seraph of this millennium, absorbing King Araqiel, and Mammon blood flowing through Camio. The Old Gods were unaware of Wolf's transformation, but theregeneration process was slow. Her body was taking much longer to reach its maximum potential. I could see that The Wolf was in no shape to battle the Old Gods, and if they learned of Camio's lineage they would do whatever it took to stop him, including stripping Wolf of her newly absorbed power and making her their puppet once more. She would be forced to do what the original Seraph had done: absorb Mammon once again.

All at once the vision disappeared, and I fell to my knees in a cold sweat. The cattail reeds were all around me once more. I caught my breath and looked up at her.

"So, you want me to hunt him down?" I huffed. "Well, fat chance of that. The last time I encountered him, he absorbed Meridian and traveled through time."

"Yes, I felt that activity as well, but you have something that can aid you in your hunt."

Wolf pointed at the sheath that now held Grus. "It would seem the Grand Elder has given you hope," she said. "Find Camio and destroy him before the Old Gods find out who he truly is. I should be at full strength in one month's time. Do this for me, Tyler, and I promise to bring Marie back, when my power is complete. Do we have a deal?"

The Wolf put out her hand. I still wasn't sure. My mind raced with all the information she had just laid on me. This felt like a trap. She could have been lying about everything just to deceive me again. I knew I should consult Marie's family first. But I was angry and heartbroken, and I missed Marie so much.

Impulsively, I took Wolf's hand, sealing the deal. It was a brash decision, but if it would bring back Marie... I'd take those odds.

Twilight descended on the town as I strode through the cattails, back to the inn. Outside of the taverns, people were laughing and chattering, the soft glow of lamplight punctuating the darkness. I was exhausted and made my way back to my room, slipping past the dining room, where my in-laws were drinking. In my room, I kicked off my shoes and laid on top of the sheets, closing my eyes. I contemplated my agreement with Wolf, hoping I had made the right choice. Almost imperceptibly, I fell into a dreamless sleep.

I woke in the soft light of early dawn. The inn was silent. A glowing light was streaming under my door. *Oh boy,* I thought, *what now?* Eerie glowing lights and Demons were never a good combination. Rousing myself from sleep, I walked toward the door, unsure of what would happen next. Cautiously, I opened my door to find a glowing ring in the hallway. I stared at it, still half-asleep and not quite sure what to do.

Moments later, out of the ring stepped the Flower, battle-worn and covered in dirt and what might have been dried blood – his or someone else's, I couldn't say.

"Get dressed, Merozantine," whispered the Flower. "We have work to do. Camio's doing some serious damage."

What, already? I thought, *Man, that guy works fast!*

"She's right, ya know," came a familiar voice from just past the light. "It's time to get to work, sweets."